Dedicated to the America

that once was

Su Casa Es Mi Casa

Frank Kyle

2016 Revised Edition

Cover design by Todd Engel, Engel Creative

The day begins much like any other day, with my reading the newspaper. And then the doorbell rings. I go and open the door. Before me stands a short, dark brown, thickly built woman holding an infant in her arms. My wife, Anne, arrives and gives me a questioning look because no one like the woman lives in the neighborhood. For a moment the three of us stand in silence looking at one another. Anne and I wait for the woman to say something, but she just stands there silently. Finally I say, "Can I help you." She responds in Spanish, which I don't understand. I shake my head and say, "No *comprenday*." Then she says, "*No tengo casa*," and then apparently attempts to elaborate in a flood of Spanish, which again neither Anne nor I understand.

I turn to Anne, who gives me a nervous look, and then turn back to the woman, who continues talking to us in Spanish. I can hear desperation in her voice, but I don't understand a word and she just keeps talking. I let out a sigh. *Why doesn't she shut up! Doesn't she realize that we don't understand?* Then the baby starts crying. She has awakened the baby. I noticed her hand moving under the baby's blanket just before it started crying, and every time her hand moves the baby lets out a whine. *She's pinching the baby!* Suddenly the baby is having a crying fit. *Jesus Christ, what's going on?* I turn to Anne, who looks at me with raised eyebrows as if to say, *Do something, Jeffrey!*

"What do you want me to do?" I ask.

"Tell her to go away. I don't want her here. She looks like a Gypsy. I don't trust her. Something's not right." I'm thinking the same thing and feel myself becoming nervous, but I am not sure whether it's because of the woman or because of Anne.

"Sorry, we can't help you. Sorry. Go away!" I say and start to close the door.

Then the woman begins to let out a strange high-pitched yell. "*Aiheee! Aiheee!*" She isn't crying; there are no tears. It's a wail of some kind, a wail of exasperation perhaps. The combination of the woman's wailing and the baby's crying creates a tremendous racket. I look beyond the woman to see if any of the neighbors have come to investigate the noise, but the street's empty. Finally I shake my head and say, "No, no. Please go away. We can't help you."

"*We ... can ... not ... help ... you,*" I say very deliberately, but she pays me no attention. It's as if she is in some kind of trance.

"*Aiheee! Aiheee! Aiheee! Aiheee! Aiheee!*" she continues, the wails growing louder and more rhythmic, finally becoming a chant. *JESUS CHRIST!* flashes in my mind like a Las Vegas neon. Now the woman's baby is crying in unison with the wails of its mother, the cacophony becoming unbearable. Just for a moment I think the baby is a midget and this whole thing is a setup, like the time when a woman with two kids walked up to me in a mini-mall parking lot and said that she was stranded and needed money to get back home, which of course was some place hundreds of miles away like Fresno. Though I knew I was being duped, I asked her how much money she needed, thinking she would say something like five dollars. But no, she said she needed fifty dollars but that seventy-five would be even more helpful because she and her children could buy something to eat on way back home. I stared at her in disbelief then turned and walked away as she hurled expletives at me in front of her children. I thought *you can't go anywhere anymore without encountering beggars or con artists of one kind or another. What's the country coming to?*

Back to the present, Anne puts her face near mine and says, "Jeffrey, for God's sake just do something... Just shut the door."

So I try shutting the door, gently but firmly because the woman has crossed the threshold and is pushing against the door while holding the baby that is still screaming at the top of its lungs between herself and the door. But the door gives only a little and then won't budge. I give it a big push, forcing the woman back. I feel a sense of relief as the door almost shuts, but then it stops. *Damn it!* I push again but it won't close any further. *Why is the damn thing stuck?* I push harder and suddenly the woman lets out a terrific yell and begins screaming "*Aiheee! Aiheee! Aiheee! Aiheee! Aiheee! Aiheee! Aiheee! Aiheee!*" *What the hell!* I look down and see that she has her foot wedged between the door and frame. *No wonder she's screaming!*

So I open the door slightly and in a begging voice say, "Go away, please. Please go away." My face is no more than six inches from hers, but she continues to scream, "*Aiheee! Aiheee! Aiheee! Aiheee!*" and then gives the door a great shove, which catches me off guard and allows her to squeeze back in between the door and the frame. Becoming desperate I push on her face with the palm of my hand, pushing her head backwards until it must be touching her back. Still her body won't move. *She'd allow me to break her neck before she'd back off.*

Next I put the full weight of my shoulder against the door. But she doesn't budge and the baby continues to scream full throttle. Then the woman starts wiggling forward like a pit bull trying to get in. *If I push on the door any harder I'll crush the baby. Then the cops will come and arrest me for infanticide.*

"What's going on, Jeffrey?" Anne asks as she tries to look over my shoulder. Suddenly she shouts, "Just shut the goddamn door." Shocked by her tone of voice, I turn to her. She has the expression of someone who had just seen a ghost. *What the hell!* I look back at the woman. Eyes wide open and wearing a fiendish, determined grin, she strains against the door. *Yeah, she is kind of scary.*

Looking back at Anne while struggling with the door, I say, "That's what I'm trying to do, Anne, but I can't. The woman won't budge and the baby is between her and the door. Do you want me to crush the baby?"

"Oh my God, she's mad!"

"No, I think she's desperate," though I immediately think that she could be both desperate and mad.

Our daughter walks in and says, "What going on? Why all the yelling? Dad, what are you doing?"

"There's a mad woman trying to get into the house," Anne tells her. Kelly then comes up and squeezes in as much as she can between me and her mother. What she sees is the woman and baby both screaming to high hell. *Aiheee, aiheee, waaah, waaah, waaah, aiheee, aiheee, waaah, waaah, waaah, aiheee, aiheee*. The noise has become unbearable.

"God she has a kid with her and she's pushing on the door with it. She's crazy, Dad. Shut the door and call the police. They'll do something. Dad, *shut the door!*"

"I can't, Kelly. Can't you see the kid?"

"Yeah, but what are you going to do, spend the whole day in a shoving match with her? Who is she anyway?"

"I don't know." Then I see a door across the street open and a man in either a bathing suit or in his boxer shorts looking at us. A woman at the same house stares through a window. Another woman appears with her dog. *Jesus! The whole neighborhood is watching.* Then the racket suddenly stops. *What a relief.* I look at the woman and she stares back at me. Her baby is asleep. I'm thinking *this is impossible.*

"I am lost, please help me," she says in English.

"I thought you couldn't speak English," I say.

"Just a little." I hear Kelly laugh behind me. "I don't believe this," she says.

"May I come in for a little bit?" I sigh and turn to Anne.

"She wants to come in."

"Jeffrey, that's not a good idea."

"She says just for a little bit."

"How is it she's now fluent in English?"

"I don't know. Do I let her in?"

"Daaaad!" says Kelly, "she's already in." I turn back and there she is standing next to Kelly.

"Listen lady..."

"My name is Imelda and this is my baby Aniceto. I am very sorry to disturb you, but my husband is coming for me."

"I thought you said you were lost."

"Not exactly. I'm looking for my home."

"You don't know where your home is? How can that be?"

"My husband knows and he's coming here to get me. Very soon my husband will come."

"Her English is pretty good," Kelly chimes in. "I thought I'd have a chance to use my Spanish."

"He's coming here? I don't understand." She ignores me and turns to Kelly.

"Do you speak Spanish?" the woman asks Kelly.

"Yes, some. I studied Spanish in high school."

"That's very good. You will find it very useful."

"That's what my Spanish teacher said. 'If you take Latin,' he said 'who are you going to talk to? All the Latin speakers are dead. If you take French, when will you use it? Only when you eat at a French restaurant. But here in San Diego you can use Spanish every day, everywhere.'"

"Your Spanish teacher is a very smart man."

"I guess so, but..."

"Hey guys, I hate to interrupt but let's get back to the problem at hand."

"Yes, Señor Thomas, that's a very good idea. I would like to tell you my situation."

"You know my name. How do you know my name?"

"I asked a girl outside who lived in this house and she said Jeffrey Thomas and his family."

"Why did you do that?"

"I stopped in front of your house because it is a very nice house and the little girl was playing next door, so I asked her."

"I still don't get it. Why did you come to our house?"

"Like I said it is a very nice house and I thought you would help me. Was I wrong, Señor Thomas?"

"I don't know. If you need money to get to your husband, I'll give you money. I'll even call you a cab."

"No, no, no. I don't know where he is. We've just arrived."

"Arrived?"

"Yes, and my husband has relatives who will help us."

"Help you to do what? I thought you were trying to get to your house."

"Yes, that's true. I mean to help us with the car."

"I see. But how did you get *here*?"

"I walked."

"You and your husband walked?"

"Yes."

"I thought you had a problem with your car?"

"Yes, yes."

"*Yes, yes* what?"

"The car, it broke down, Señor Thomas."

"So you walked from where?"

"From the border."

"The Mexican border?"

"Yes, that's it."

"Are you here illegally?"

"No, no, just for work and to visit my husband's family."

"Family? I don't know about this. It all sounds pretty shady to me."

"No, no. It's not shady. You must help me." And then she started screeching again. "*Aiheee! Aiheee! Aiheee! Aiheee!*"

"No don't start that again, please. I can't think while you're doing that."

"Dad, what are you doing? Just tell her to leave."

"Kelly, what do you think I am trying to do?"

"I don't know, Dad. What *are* you trying to do?"

"I'm trying to figure out what's going on."

"I'm calling the police," says Anne. Well that really sets off Imelda.

"*Aiheee! Aiheee! Aiheee! Aiheee!*" Then the baby starts crying "*waaah, waaah, waaah.*"

"Okay, everyone just shut up for a second. I need to think. We can find a solution to this problem." Then the woman walks over to the sofa and opens her blouse and starts nursing the baby and talking to it in Spanish.

"I'll feed the baby while you think, Señor Thomas."

"The baby's kind of cute, huh Dad?" says Kelly. I glare at her. Anne has her hand to her face as if she is wiping away a cobweb. She does that when she gets really frustrated. Finally I go over to the woman and sit next to her so that I won't be staring at her breast, which has poured out when she unbuttoned her blouse.

"Listen... uhh, Imelda. I think we can help you. You need to meet up with your husband, but you don't know where he is and you have no one to call. What about his relatives? Could you call them?"

"No, no, I can't. I don't know the number."

"We could call information and get their number."

"They don't have a phone. They use the pay phone at the store to call us."

"Well, let's see, uhh... uhh" I stammer as I try to think of something. "You know the police could really help in this matter. The police are not the Border Patrol. They will not arrest you if you are here illegally. In fact they don't want to know about any of that. They would just help you."

I am not really sure that is the case but to be honest I don't care if they call the Border Patrol. I know that sounds cold-hearted but I even thought of dragging her out of the house, but didn't. I mean what's more sacred than a mother and child?

Kelly and Anne stand silently. They look at Imelda and then at me, expecting a decision, as if I'm the man-of-the-house, which I am.

"When do you expect your husband back, Imelda?" I ask, glancing at Anne, who seems displeased by the question.

"He will be here anytime."

"Hmm. Are you sure?"

"Yes, I am certain."

I turn to Anne and say, "I suppose she could wait here for him." I smile looking for some sympathy. Anne walks off into the kitchen the door swinging shut behind her.

"What's wrong with your mother?" I ask Kelly.

"What do you think, *Dad*? You're going let this woman stay here, aren't you?"

"Just until her husband returns."

"I'm going to check on Mom," she says and leaves the room.

I turn to Imelda and notice that the baby has fallen asleep, its head lying between her breasts, one partly covered, the other in full view. Imelda looks at me with grateful adoration like a puppy. I think to myself *why doesn't she cover the exposed breast*. I know a nursing woman's breast should be seen only as a source of food for a baby and not as a sexual object, and I'm trying very hard not to see it that way, not having much luck.

Maybe in her village the women go topless, like Tahitians before the Europeans arrived and spoiled all the fun, and the men of the village pay them no mind. But this is San Diego, city of porn shops and strip bars. I've never been to either but I admit a few times I've been tempted to go to the latter just to see what they're like. But I always thought they're probably like the bar in the *Sopranos*, young women twisting like snakes around metal poles to sultry music while men of all ages wearing sick looks stare at them as if under a voodoo spell. One such place in Point Loma is called The Animal Farm. The name seems appropriate. Some things will never change. Perhaps they can't, which is a really depressing thought.

"Imelda!" I say almost shouting, realizing I had fallen under the spell of her breast.

"Yes, Señor Thomas," she says, startled by my sudden outburst.

"Your husband should be here any time, yes?"

"Yes, that's right. He should be here any moment." I go to the front door and open it, hoping that he would be standing there but of course he isn't. Not only that, it's dark outside. *Where did the day go?* I return to Imelda and tell her that it's getting late, that she might as well spend the night. You can sleep on the couch. I'll bring you blankets and pillows"

"Gracias, Señor Thomas, I'm very sorry to be such a bother. I'll wait here."

"Yes, of course."

After giving Imelda blankets and two pillows I leave her sitting on the couch smiling gratefully and go to the bedroom, take off my clothes and get into bed next to Anne who seems to have already fallen asleep. Lying in bed, I look at the dim light coming through the open door and think I've made a big mistake allowing Imelda into our home. Then she appears in the doorway. She has followed me to the bedroom. She begins to remove her clothes. All I can see is the silhouette of her body. She approaches and climbs into bed next to me. I move away closer to Anne. Fortunately we have a king-size bed. None of this seems to awaken Anne. I wonder where Imelda has put her baby. I also wonder if Anne is really asleep but I don't move, only lie quietly thinking about the big mess I have made of the whole affair.

The next day I find Imelda waiting on the sofa, her baby in her lap. She smiles when I enter the room. I begin to blush and look away. Anne and Kelly are also in the room, Kelly sitting in one of the chairs, Anne pacing about. Finally she stops and says, "Jeffrey, we've waited a day and a night for her husband to show up but he hasn't come. How long is this going to continue?"

"Her husband will be here anytime. Just be patient," I say.

"How do you know that? Is that what *she* told you? Have you forgotten that's what she said yesterday? *Be patient*? The woman spent the night in our bed for God's sake. *Be patient*! You must be mad."

"Señora Thomas, I'm very grateful to you for allowing me to stay in your home and to sleep in your bed."

"I bet you are," Anne snaps back.

"Anne, please. Let's try to remain cool."

"Señora, there's no reason to be angry. Señor Thomas did nothing."

"What is she talking about, Jeffrey?"

"Nothing. She's just trying to calm you down."

Kelly gets up from her chair and announces, "You two are pathetic. I'm going to my room," and storms out.

I turn to Anne. She looks at me angrily. Then I turn to Imelda, who smiles sweetly. *Why must she smile like that? God!* Suddenly I feel a wave of abhorrence sweep over me.

Then there's a knock at the door. "He's here! My husband is here," Imelda says joyfully.

"Thank God," says Anne.

I go to the door and open it. A dark little boy and girl holding hands stand in front of me. "Who are you?" I ask. But they do not respond.

I turn to Imelda, who is now standing next to me holding my hand. I remove my hand from hers and ask, "Do you know these children?" But before she can answer the children cry, "Mamma, Mamma" and hurry to her, hugging her and talking in Spanish. Anne lets out a sarcastic laugh and walks back to the living room. I turn to Imelda.

"Imelda, are these your children?"

"Yes, yes, they are. Aren't they beautiful?"

Under the circumstance I don't see them as beautiful, but say "Yes, they are beautiful. But what about their father? Where is he?"

"Oh they are not my present husband's children. They are children of my second husband, who remains in Mexico."

"You're divorced?"

"Not exactly."

"You have two husbands!"

"Yes, in a way, but my second husband could not come with us."

"I don't really want to know any more about your marital situation, Imelda. Tell me, who is the father of the baby?"

"My husband, of course."

"The one we are waiting for."

"Yes, yes, in a way."

"In a way?" *JESUS CHRIST!* "Forget about who's the father of the baby. Is one of your husbands here? That's what I want to know." Imelda then speaks in Spanish to the children.

"Yes, he is here and will soon arrive."

"Arrive?" I look up and down the street but see no one. "What do you mean he's here but hasn't yet arrived?"

"He is close by and will soon arrive here," she says.

I feel tired and wish I could lie down just for a while. I close the door and walk back into the living room. I begin to explain to Anne but she says, "I heard. So what are you going to do, Jeffrey? There are now more of them than there are of us. What are you going to do? We just can't have them stay here. *This* can't continue."

"I know, I know. Let's wait until her husband comes. He'll be here any minute. Isn't that right, Imelda?"

"Yes, Señor Thomas." I hate the way she addresses me, but say nothing.

"*Ooo-kay*, let's wait. *Hey*, these children look hungry. What about fixing them something to eat?" I say this as cheerily as I can but know it must have sounded hollow to Anne, since it did to me.

"We're very hungry," says the little boy.

"You speak English?" I ask.

"Not too good, but some."

"Hmm," I murmur.

"They're your children, Jeffrey, why don't *you* feed them," Anne says, apparently steamed by my suggestion.

"What do you mean they are *my* children?"

"You let this woman into our home and now these children."

"What else could I do?" I respond lamely.

"You could try being the-man-of-the-house."

I can see that she's really... well, pissed off. She's never said anything like that to me before. Turning to the children, she says, "Come into the kitchen you two. I'll make you sandwiches." She then walks away, Imelda's children following behind.

Imelda returns to the sofa. I follow and sit in a chair across from her. At the moment I can't face either Anne or Kelly, so I watch Imelda, looking for some clue as to what is going on. She smiles sweetly and opens her blouse for the baby to feed but the baby is still asleep. She holds her breast as if to offer it to the baby but the baby is still fast asleep. I watch mesmerized. Is she trying to bewitch me or simply repay me for my kindness?

I think I must have fallen asleep because I seem to hear a voice in a dream.

"What in the fuck are you doing, Jeffrey?!!!" It's Anne's voice and I'm no longer dreaming. I awake and find myself sitting next to Imelda.

"I was dreaming I was nursing."

"Nursing! Jesus Christ, have you lost your mind? No wonder you don't want this woman to leave."

"I'm sorry. I don't know what has come over me."

"She's a fucking witch! She's got you under her spell."

"Hey bitch, don't you call my mother a fucking witch or else I'll cut your throat while you sleep tonight." We both turn to the little boy.

"What did he say?" Anne asks, her eyes opening wide with shock.

"Gonzalo, you shut your mouth. These good people saved your mama. Say you're sorry."

"I'm sorry. I'm sorry. I really am sorry." Then the little boy starts sobbing uncontrollably.

"What's happening?" Anne asks, still very much dazed by the boy's outburst and now by his sobbing.

"You must forgive him, Señora Thomas. He has seen bad things."

"Bad things?" Anne says in an inquisitive tone of voice, though I don't think she really wants an answer.

"Bad things in Mexico."

"Don't say any more. I don't want to know. I'm sorry that he has seen bad things but I really don't want to know about them. I'll be upstairs, Jeffrey," she says as she leaves the room.

I was right. She didn't want to know. I get up wearily and walk to the front door and open it. It's dark. I turn to Imelda. He's not coming, is he, Imelda?"

"He will come, Señor Thomas. I promise."

"It's just I don't think my family can take much more of your being here."

"I understand. He will come. I promise."

"Perhaps it's time that we all go to bed," I suggest. At this Imelda's children go to her and say something in Spanish.

"They're afraid to sleep in the living room, Señor Thomas."

"They can sleep on the floor in Kelly's room."

"I won't sleep in the same room with them," Kelly says. I look over toward the kitchen where Kelly is standing. *Jesus Christ, did she see me asleep next to Imelda?* I don't ask. I don't want to know. The little girl begins to cry and Kelly says she'll sleep downstairs on the sofa. So I follow Imelda and her children to Kelly's room where Imelda fixes the two children a bed on the floor.

I then go to our room and lie down next to Anne but I can't sleep. After a few minutes of staring into the darkness I get up to go to the bathroom. As I start back toward the bedroom I hear a "shiss, shiss." It's Imelda. She's standing naked in front of her door. "Come here, Señor Thomas." I walk over to her and she takes my hands puts one on her breast and the other between her legs.

"I am very grateful to you, Señor Thomas. Come with me for a while. I am afraid."

I feel terrorized. Perhaps Anne is right that she is a witch. I've read that sorcery and witchcraft are practiced in parts of Mexico. I pull away saying that I appreciate her gratitude but that I'm a married man.

"I'm a married woman, Señor Thomas. Twice."

"Good night, Imelda."

The next morning I find Anne sitting at the kitchen table and it's obvious that she's been crying.

"I'm sorry, honey," I tell her. "I don't know what is happening. I'm just trying to do the right thing. I love you, baby."

"Jeffrey, don't talk to me right now. You make me sick and your excuses only make it worse. You let those people take over Kelly's room! Just get them out of our house or I'll leave with Kelly."

"I'll do that. I promise." I go into the living room where I find Imelda with her baby and the two children sitting quietly.

"He called, Señor Thomas. He'll be here soon."

"Thank God, but I didn't hear the phone ring."

"It rang only once, in the middle of the night, and I answered it right away so you and your wife would not be disturbed."

"Thanks loads for thinking about us." I return to Anne and give her the good news. She gives me a suspicious look.

"Do you know where Kelly is?"

"No. Did she go out? Call Shannon. She's probably there." I stand before her for a moment waiting for a response.

"I'll call Shannon," she says. "Shouldn't you get back to entertaining your guests?" The contempt in her voice is unbearable so I go back into the living room, where Imelda, her children, and I continue to wait for her husband.

After what seems an eternity there's a knock at the door. I go and open it. Facing me is a short, dark man wearing a mustache and looking a lot like Pancho Villa. *So this is the man we've been waiting for.*

I turn to Imelda. "I believe your husband is here." She gets up from the sofa, baby in arm, and comes to the door, her children following closely behind. None of them show much enthusiasm. What I feel is a dull sense of relief. I step aside and open the door so that Imelda can see her husband. Imelda walks up and examines the man as if she were identifying a suspect in a lineup. Then she says, "Yes, this is my husband." I'm thinking *these people are a mystery.*

"Well, I guess you all will be on your way," I say, but she ignores me and starts talking to him in Spanish. It's then that I notice an older boy with him, about sixteen or seventeen. He's taller than Pancho and gives me a stern, unfriendly look. *Why is he giving me a dirty look? I'm the one whose life has been turned upside down. And why didn't I see him before.* After a minute of intense discussion with her husband Imelda turns to me and asks if they can come in for a few minutes.

"Oh, Imelda, I would rather *they not come in.* Does he need money for gas?"

"Oh no, Señor Thomas, you have already been too kind. But he wants to thank you for helping me and to explain what happened." Her expression is both pleading and grateful. I look at Pancho and he smiles and seems a lot more friendly than his young companion. I turn back to Imelda.

"I don't think so, Imelda. You know my family is already very angry with me."

"Thank you, thank you, Señor Thomas." Then the baby begins to cry. "The baby is hungry. I must feed him."

"I think you misunderstand, Imelda," I say.

"*Muchas gracias*, Señor Thomas," says her husband.

"*You* also know my name?" I say surprised, though I know I shouldn't be. Then he says something in Spanish to Imelda. She looks over at me and asks if he can see his child. And before I can protest that he has just seen him, she walks back to the sofa, sits down, opens her blouse and once again exposes her breast.

Astonished, I stare at her. A wave of guilt sweeps over me. What have I done? She is a sorceress who has taken control of my home. Had her husband come first I would not have allowed him into the house. But Imelda... Well she's a Mexican Trojan Horse. I look over at the father wondering if he can read my thoughts. No. His look is very friendly. He obviously has had a difficult time during the past few days and is happy to be reunited with his wife and child.

"*Mío niño*," he says smiling proudly.

"He wants to see his baby, Señor Thomas."

"Okay but he can't stay. You must leave." Then I feel the door being pushed open by her husband, not hard but with a steady, irresistible pressure. I look at him and he smiles again, but his eyes now seem less friendly.

"What's going on now?" Anne has entered the room. I turn to her as the two men come in and walk over to Imelda. The younger man sits down in one of the chairs. He looks even older than before, perhaps nineteen or twenty years of age.

"I'm glad you have everything under control, Jeffrey, you stupid fuck!" The tone of Anne's language shocks me. I can't recall her ever speaking to me that way. In fact she has never used the word *fuck* before Imelda arrived.

"Jeffrey, who are these two men?"

"Calm yourself, Anne. He's the husband we've been waiting for. He's here to take Imelda and the children."

"The children don't seem too excited to see their daddy," she says in a sarcastic tone of voice. I look over. They're sitting quietly on the floor staring at Anne and me.

"He's not their father," says Imelda flatly.

"Well they don't seem very excited about seeing their step-father," Anne says.

"They are still tired from the long journey," says Imelda.

"Of course," I say. "Well, anyway, we're happy to see him, aren't we, Anne?"

"That depends, Jeffrey. Right now they are in our house, sitting very comfortably in our living room. When they are gone, all of them, then I'll be happy."

"I understand, Anne."

"And who is the other man?"

"I don't know, perhaps his son."

"Do something, Jeffrey! Just do something about all this, and do it *quick*. Otherwise I'm calling the police." Then she turns and takes a couple of steps toward the kitchen but then walks back to the living room and studies the family as if looking for something. What that is I do not know. She looks back at me then walks to the door of the kitchen where she stands with her arms folded. I believe it's the first time I've seen hatred in my wife's eyes. I walk over to Imelda.

"Imelda, you all must leave. Pleeease leave."

"Arsenio is very happy to see his child. And he wants me to tell you he is very grateful to you for taking care of us."

"I'm glad to have been able to help but did you hear my wife? She is very angry with me for allowing you to stay, so you must go. All of you."

"We will. I promise, but there is one problem."

"Money? I will give you money."

"Thank you, Señor Thomas, but we could never take money from you. You've been too good to us."

"Well what is the problem then?"

"The car is not yet fixed, but it will soon be." As she says this Arsenio nods in agreement, and I wonder if he understands English.

"Will it be fixed today?" I ask.

"Yes, it should be." Again Arsenio nodded in agreement.

"*Should* be?" I repeat.

"It should be. The car was taken to a cousin who is a mechanic. He said he'd start work on the car right away."

"What is the problem with the car?"

"Nothing serious but we don't want it to break down on the way to L.A."

"Look, Imelda, could you all stay at your cousin's house?"

"Oh no, Señor Thomas, it is small and his family is very large."

"I see." For just a moment I think that I should give them my car. I could sign it over to them, but I reject the idea as ridiculous. A feeling of confusion and apathy sweeps over me. Then I hear a noise. It's Anne. She has returned to the living room.

"Well, Jeffrey. Do you have everything under control?" The first thing I think is she's being sarcastic but I'm not sure. *God I don't have the heart to tell her the truth.* Or maybe I am just afraid to tell her the truth. I need to relax. If only I could lie down and close my eyes just for a little while.

"Yes," I finally say, "we're just waiting on their car."

"Their car? How did *they* get here?" I look to Imelda for the answer.

"They were dropped off by the man who is fixing the car." Again Arsenio nodded in agreement.

"Oh, Jeffrey," she says in a deploring tone of voice and walks backs to the kitchen.

"The baby is wet. I must change his diaper," Imelda says, and then gets up and walks upstairs to Kelly's room. I haven't seen Kelly and assume she is staying with a friend until this thing blows over. I watch Imelda go up the stairs. The two men and the two children sit quietly staring at me.

"I'll be back. I need to talk to Imelda," I say then leave the living room and go upstairs.

When I walk in I find Imelda on the opposite side of the bed facing me as she changes the baby's diaper. Both of her breasts, as large pineapples, hang out of her blouse, almost touching the baby. The dark nipples are wide and the breasts sway back and forth as she cleans the baby and puts on a new diaper. The motion makes me dizzy. Then she removes the comforter and makes a bed on the floor for the baby. After placing the baby on the comforter she walks over and sits down in front of me. Both her breasts are still exposed. She smiles sweetly at me and shyly places both her hands on the insides of her knees her knees, causing her arms to push her breasts together and outward. I feel myself beginning to hyperventilate. Then she lies back on the bed and looks at me.

Has she fallen in love with me? Her face seems drawn to mine. The expression is both loving and seductive. Her blouse opens further and her breasts spread outward until each one is as round as her head. I notice now that her waist is quite trim and that what I had taken for a stocky build was caused by her breasts. She reaches out to me like a mother to her child and draws me to her. I lean toward her. She takes my head in her hands and pulls me to her breasts. My god, what is happening to me? I jerk back in a paroxysm of fear. What if Anne or Kelly saw me! My god!

"*Mi pequeño hombre*" she says and then begins to softly to sing a song in Spanish, a lullaby. I recall the John Keats poem *La Belle Dame Sans Merci* in which a knight is seduced from his duty by a wood nymph and later he awakes to find himself alone, wretched and lost.

"Jeffrey, Jeffrey! Wake up! Wake up, damn it." It's Anne, shaking me and yelling frantically.

"What is it? What is it?" I mumble still half asleep.

"Get up! Jeffrey. I'll be in the kitchen." I notice I'm in Kelly's bed. Then I remember Imelda but she's not there. *Thank God!* Then I think, *Oh God, what happened?* Here I am asleep in my daughter's bedroom while those Mexicans interlopers have taken over my home. The thought of what I have allowed to happen sickens me. *What a fool I've been!* Anne hasn't left the room. She stands over me, looking at me with an expression of wonderment as if she had just found an alien in her daughter's room. No, the expression isn't wonderment but disgust. I recall Kafka's *The Metamorphosis*, a story that describes a son who turns into a cockroach. Before that metamorphosis he was his family's provider. But he didn't choose to become a disgusting insect but I did. Now I understand the expression on Anne's face. She turns and walks out of the room.

"I'm coming, I'm coming," I say in a pathetic tone of voice as she disappears from view. *Oh, Anne!* I put on my pants and shirt and leave the room. I must speak to her. But as soon as I walk out of the room I see what has upset her so. **Graffiti** everywhere. **Graffiti** has been sprayed on the walls and ceiling. I go to the bathroom and **Graffiti** has been scratched into the mirror and sink, into the porcelain of the bathtub. It's even been carved into the toilet seat. At first I feel disoriented as if I'm in the wrong house. But I'm not and I begin to realize that what I'm looking at is a nightmare of my own creation. I feel sick, sick with anger and hatred.

As I go down the stairs to find Anne a sharp pain suddenly cuts into my hand. *Goddamn it that hurt!* I look and see a large splinter sticking into the pad of my small finger. The wound begins to turn purple under the skin and a drop of blood forms at the entrance of the wound. The banister has been crudely carved into as if with the rough blade of a hatchet. As I pull out the splinter the pain causes me to wince. *Goddamn it fuck!* I say under my breath. I want to fucking scream, but I don't. At the bottom of the steps I look toward the living room. All six of our visitors are still there. All but Imelda stare at me with blank zombie faces.

Imelda smiles. She has one breast exposed even though the baby isn't nursing. When our eyes meet, she holds the breast up as if to offer it to me. I feel disgusted, not so much with her as with myself. Then I notice her husband watching me. *What is he thinking? What is going on? What in the HELL am I doing? I've got to get a hold of myself. These people have invaded and trashed my home.* I hurry off to the kitchen where I find Anne weeping. I walk up behind her and take hold of her shoulders.

"It's okay Anne. It's okay." She jerks away and glares at me, then yells, "It's not okay, *Jeffrey!* It's not fucking okay. Look! Look around. What do you see?"

I look at her shoulders. One has a spot of blood from my finger. I go to the sink and wash my hand. Then I look around. *Graffiti* has been sprayed everywhere in the kitchen. The odor of paint is overwhelming and makes me lightheaded and slightly nauseous. *Graffiti* has been carved into the doors of the refrigerator and the surface of the kitchen table.

"What does it say?"

"I don't know, Jeffrey. And I don't care what it says. You're missing the point by worrying about what it says. It probably says you're a dumb fuck for allowing a bunch of Mexican aliens to invade your home, to take it over, to trash it, and to run your daughter off. *Where is Kelly?* Have you thought about Kelly?"

"Well, yes. Where is she?"

"I don't know and you don't care. You make me sick, Jeffrey. Sick, sick, sick. You're worse than *them*. I'm calling the police right now." That last remark was cutting but she's right. *I am disgusting.*

"Do that, Anne. Call the police. You're right. Things have gotten out of hand." Anne picks up the phone and dials 911. She listens for a minute.

"This *is* a *fucking* emergency!" she yells and then begins sobbing. I take the phone from her and listen. A recording says, *"If this is not an emergency, call the police station. Otherwise stay on the line. Your call is very important to us and will be answered in the order in which it was received."* I wait. The recording repeats. *Fuck!*

"Maybe I should drive to the police station and report what's going on."

"And leave me here alone with these fucking people?"

"You could come with me."

"And what about Kelly? What if Kelly comes home? She will be here all alone. You must be kidding. Look what they've done to the house. Jesus fucking Christ, Jeffrey, can't you see what's happening?"

"Did you call Shannon?"

"Yes, but there was no answer. I've called all her friends that I have numbers for but all I get is a busy signal or no answer. Oh Jeffrey, what's going on?" And she begins to sob again.

"Okay, Anne. You stay on the phone. I'm sure a 911 operator will be available soon. I'm going to talk with the family. I'll talk with Imelda. I think she'll listen to me."

"I bet she will," Anne responds sarcastically.

"What do you mean by that remark?" I ask, feeling insulted.

"Try to be a husband and father and get them out of our home."

"I will, I will," I say, feeling deeply wounded by her words.

"Be careful, Jeffrey. You're a fucking jerk but I still love you. Though right now I'm not sure why. If Kelly's okay, I will forgive you all this."

I smile to her. "I love you too." *But what if Kelly isn't okay? What have I done?* I leave the kitchen, feeling anxious and nauseous. My mood is one of anger. The fucking **graffiti** is everywhere. In the living room the family is sitting just as I left them.

"Imelda!" I say sharply.

"Yes, Jeffrey?" she responds in that sweet, adoring voice that now sickens me. I see that it was all a ruse and I was her sucker. And who in the hell does she think she is calling me by my first name?

"Look at what your family has done to my house. You've turned it into a fucking nightmare! *And don't call me Jeffrey!*"

"Señor, do not speak in that tone of voice to my wife," Arsenio says in a menacing tone of voice. I turn to him.

"So you speaka English. Why am I not surprised? I want you and your family to get out of my house." Arsenio jumps to his feet and approaches me with such ferocity that I think he is going to attack me but instead he sticks his face so close to mine that I can smell the alcohol on his breath.

"You enjoy my wife's titties and make a whore out of her..."

"What do you mean?" I ask shocked by the accusation.

"Señor Thomas, do you think I am a fool? Do you think I am blind? I see what you do. I see how you look at Imelda's titties. And she has told me about you. How you came to where she was sleeping and placed your hand on her titty and grab her pussy..."

"She did that. I didn't."

"You need not lie, Señor Thomas. Imelda is irresistible and I do not begrudge what you do. I am a generous man. I give my wife's beautiful titties as a gift because I know you desire them and also I see that you own wife is pale and dried up..."

"Arsenio, leave my wife out of this."

"You wish I leave your wife out of this but you cannot take your eyes off mine. I see lust in them yet I have no desire to fuck your wife. She's too pale and dried up for my taste and I will say no more about *her*. But I give you Imelda, a gift for your hospitality. So you will not tell us to leave until we are ready. No, no, you, who have made a whore of my wife, will not tell us when we must leave. And as long as we are here you may have Imelda."

"I have not made a whore of her. If anything she has been trying to seduce me. And I will tell you to leave my house because it is *my* house, not yours." Saying this I turn to Imelda, who smiles sweetly and holds her breast out to me..."

"Look for yourself, Arsenio."

"Of course she offers her titty to you. It is a token of her gratitude but I also think that she would not do such a thing in front of all of us had you not already accepted her affection."

For just a moment I think that Arsenio is not so unreasonable. What kind of man would allow his wife to offer her breast to another man? Most men would be violently angry with me and Imelda. Certainly his language toward me is hostile and disrespectful but why should he respect me? He has every reason to believe I have been with his wife. Arsenio is right. Why should I deserve to be spoken to with respect? Who am I? Nothing. I goggle at his wife like an adolescent looking at dirty pictures. I fail to protect my family. And still he offers his wife to me. But what about the **graffiti**? How does he explain that?

"It is true. I have acted shamefully toward Imelda. I don't know why I have behaved in that way but now I apologize for my behavior..."

"You did it, Señor Thomas, because you desire her big titties. I understand, Señor Thomas. I too am a man. Look at them, Señor Thomas. Look!" I look. Imelda has put the baby on her lap and opened her blouse exposing both of her breasts.

"You see, Señor Thomas, they are still there, there for you and for me. I am not a selfish man, Señor Thomas. Is that not why God gave a woman two titties, so that they could be shared? Go now. Take her titties into your mouth and enjoy them. Take Imelda to the privacy of your daughter's bedroom and enjoy her fruits. I will not be angry. But don't tell me I must leave. No, no, that is not possible now."

"That's very generous of you, Arsenio, but look around, look at the house. It's been ruined. Why would you do that? How can you expect me to allow you to stay after you have done this to my house?"

"I did not do that, Señor Thomas. I would never do such a thing. I am not that kind of man."

"But then who did it?"

"My son, Lope." I turn to Lope and only then do I notice that his hands are stained with black paint. I look at his face. It's filled with hatred like that of a wild beast. I want to go to him and put my hands around his throat and choke the life out of him.

"He cannot stay in this house."

"Señor Thomas, I understand that you are angry. I too would be furious but imagine how he feels seeing you constantly staring his mother's titties..."

"Perhaps she should not expose herself."

"Do not get excited, Señor Thomas. It is obvious that she exposes herself because she likes you. She is grateful for giving her and her baby shelter, as am I. But Lope is too young to understand such things. So he came to me and asked, 'Papa, what is that man doing looking at my mother as he does? He would not unless he has taken advantage of her before you and me arrived.' I explained to him that it was necessary, that we are Señor Thomas' guests and that we owe him something. I told him that whatever he did does not matter and that his mother does not love Señor Thomas but was only allowing him to enjoy himself. 'Like a gringo pig,' he responded. Yes, yes, he is a gringo pig, but now that we are in America we must learn to live with the gringo pigs."

"That was very thoughtful of you, Arsenio" I said, my voice filled with contempt which Arsenio apparently ignored or didn't notice.

"Yes, but still Lope did not understand and said that he wanted to kill you. I told him not to say such things, that Señor Thomas loves his mother titties like his baby brother does."

I'm thinking that it must seem strange to Lope to see his mother with both her breasts exposed while we are talking. He must have notice me looking at them since he arrived. Even now I can't look in Imelda's direction without staring at her breasts. I do not want to look at them but it seems men are programmed in such a way that makes it impossible to ignore them. But that cannot be true. What about the native men who live societies such as that of the Tahitians, where women go around topless? They were not obsessed. Paul Gauguin, who painted many such women, said *"Civilization is what makes you sick."* Having taken several Polynesian child-brides and apparently infecting some of them with syphilis he himself was an example of that statement. And I seem to be no better because I realize I'm no longer looking at Arsenio as we speak but at Imelda's breasts.

"See there, Señor Thomas." I turn back to Arsenio.

"Do not be embarrassed. Take Imelda upstairs to your daughter's room and satisfy yourself. As I said I too am a man and it's not good for a man not to be satisfied. Take her."

I look at Lope. His expression is full of hatred. And why does Arsenio keep referring to the room as *my daughter's room*? To annoy me I'm sure.

"I do not want your wife. I want you and your family to leave my house."

"You've grown tired of her."

"You don't seem to understand. I haven't grown tired of her. I just don't want her. I want you to leave, all of you."

"But I have told you we cannot, not right now. We must wait for the car. And you haven't let me explain the *graffiti*. As I was about to say, Lope sprayed the house while the rest of us were asleep. But he did not spray your daughter's room because I told him to let you sleep in peace because you welcomed us into your home."

"I'm not sure *welcome* is the right word. Besides, I thought you were asleep."

"I was. This was only afterwards when I woke up. I asked Lope why he had sprayed the house and he said because he hated you. And I asked why and he said because you were always regarding his mother with disrespect. Then I ask if he sprayed the room you were in and he said no, that he was saving the best for last. And I told him that he could not spray that room, that he had done enough, that you would be very displeased when you saw what he had done, so it was better to allow you to sleep."

"Okay, okay, I get it about the *graffiti* but one thing I don't get, Arsenio, is that you say Imelda is Lope's mother and that you are his father but earlier

I'm told that you are not the father of these two children and yet the baby is your son. The whole situation looks very fishy to me."

"Nothing is fishy, Señor Thomas. As I can explain, it's all quite natural. Imelda and I were married when we were very young and she became pregnant but even before baby Lope was born I left for the United States because I knew it was the land of milk and honey. I told Imelda that I would arrange for her to come as soon as I could but life was not easy in the United States. The titties are very small and tough and one must squeeze them very hard to get just a little milk, and for a dab of honey one is stung a hundred times. So I went from job to job never making much money and always trying to stay ahead of the *la migra*. I was afraid even to mail a letter or make a phone call..."

"The what? I don't understand."

"*La migra*, you know, Immigration."

"I see. Go on."

"Well after many years passed Imelda believed that I would never return and decided to marry another man because it is not good for a son not to have a father."

"Okay so what happened? Where is the father of the two children?"

"You are an impatient man, Señor Thomas. What happened to Imelda's second husband is the tragedy of our lives of which I shall speak later but now I am trying to explain why the situation is not fishy, as you call it."

"Okay, okay. Get on with it," I say, feeling increasingly agitated by the complexity of the whole fucking mess.

Arsenio shakes his head at my impatience and continues his story. "Many years after finally getting settled in America and having a good job I am talking one day with my amigos at work during lunch when I meet this new worker, a young man who has just come to the United States..."

"Illegally?"

"Yes, of course. We all come illegally. That is the only way. Those who wait in line at the consul for their papers to be signed will be old men and women before they are allowed into the United States. So as I was saying I talk to this young man, a very good young man, and discover that he comes from my village, and he tells me that he knows Imelda..."

"And so you returned to your true love," I interject sarcastically.

"Señor Thomas, you should let me tell the story. I know my English isn't so good, though it is much better than your Spanish, so it takes a little more time for me to explain these things in English. Nevertheless an educated man like yourself should know that it is rude to interrupt another man when he is speaking. But you gringos have never been a patient people which I think causes you many problems..."

"Damn it, Arsenio," I interrupt, "the problem isn't your English and I'd say I've had too much patience with you. So get on with your story." Again shaking his head in a gesture of disapproval he continues.

"No, Señor Thomas, I did not return for Imelda for she was remarried, though she never unmarried me, but I did not care since I had remarried myself."

After all that has happened I didn't think anything further could surprise me but what Arsenio just said does. And though I know the answer I ask the question anyway. "You're married to another woman, here in the United States?"

"Of course. You especially, Señor Thomas, know a man cannot be without a woman."

I look at Imelda whose breasts are still exposed. She smiles as she always does when I look at her. Holding a breast in each hand she offers them to me. Then she sticks out her tongue, licking the air provocatively. She's beckoning me to come to her as one would gesture with the forefinger. *Disgusting! No, I'm the one who is disgusting for allowing her and her family into my home.*

"Besides, Señor Thomas, as you can see she is a whore, which she became when she married the other man. But that is nothing to me. I too still enjoy her but like you I have a wife."

"But she is the mother of your son."

"Yes, and that is why now she is here with me."

"And her second husband—did he abandon her?"

"No, no, a Mexican man will not abandon his family as gringo men do. As I was trying to tell you I returned to Mexico not for Imelda but for my son, my *hijo*."

"A little late it seems to me. He looks to be eighteen or nineteen or older."

"He looks older because life has not been easy for him but that does not matter. Blood grows thicker with time."

"I see, so you brought Imelda and your son to the United States to live with your American family?"

"Exactly. You gringos are not so stupid."

"I'm not so sure."

"No, no, you especially are very smart. You know a good thing and take it when you see it, as a man should. Imelda may be a whore, but look at those *sandías*. They are the same as when I first saw them. I could not resist them; no man can. Now many men have had them, yet they are as beautiful as when they belonged to a virgin. That is why I cannot be angry with you. You and I are alike. We are smart men. A stupid man would refuse God's gifts to men. He would say *I am a married man so must not touch the titties of another woman.* But not you and not me. We understand. We know things. You admire Imelda's gifts, which she happily offers to you, and what is the harm done? None. Her titties are beautiful and I offer them to you as gifts. And I too am happy. You scratch my back and I scratch your back, as you gringos say. You give me a house and I give you Imelda. And I think you enjoyed her more than you do your house, am I not correct? Otherwise she would not be here at this moment."

"I'd rather not talk about that and I didn't *give* you my house but allowed you stay in it for a time which is now almost up. In fact you and your family should be going."

"You are funny, Señor Thomas. Do you wish I leave Imelda with you as a housekeeper perhaps?"

"No, Arsenio, I just wish you would leave, all of you."

"I was only making a little joke, Señor Thomas. No, it's impossible that we should go at this moment. But let me finish my story about Imelda's second husband."

"Please finish your story, Arsenio," I say, feeling very, weary. I look to Imelda and her many children sitting in my living room and think *What a fucking mess I've created!*

"I will, Señor Thomas, but you must stop looking at Imelda's beautiful *sandías* and pay attention. As I said, I did not return to my homeland to find Imelda who I knew from what I had been told had become a whore. I only wanted my son to know his father and go with me to America where he has two beautiful sisters and two handsome brothers, all of whom are American citizens, not like their father and mother who traveled the long, dangerous road of thorns to paradise. We suffered as Jesus suffered and just as he finally entered Paradise so did we. Now I have brought my son who will stay in my house and be the man of the house after his father.

"But you came here illegally. Doesn't that bother you?"

"Señor Thomas, like Jesus who returned to the place from which he came so do we. The Mexican's journey to the north is a glorious return to his ancestral home taken from him by the filthy gringos who stole his land. They thought nothing of the suffering they delivered my people into just as you did not think about me when you made a whore of my first wife..."

"I did not make a whore of your first wife. For one thing you said she was already a whore."

"Let's not quibble over such a small matter. I do not resent the old thieving gringos or you, Señor Thomas, but you should not resent us. If you steal a man's property that man is not a thief if he takes it back. We Mexicans are only taking back what once belonged to us, and we do not resent the gringo but welcome him to stay among us. As you can see I do not become angry when you make a whore of my first wife. I forgive you and offer her to you."

"I wish you would stop saying that. Imelda and I did not have sex."

"Yes, I understand, like your president Jim Carter said in his confession to *Playboy*, you sinned only in your heart, perhaps many times with Imelda. But I think the sex you did not have was more like the sex your president Bill Clinton did not have with Monica Lewinsky. You Americans are a strange people. I do not think you know what you are. But you knew Imelda was my wife and did not know she had already become a whore..."

"Enough about me and Imelda and America's presidents. However I do have one question. You keep saying *sandías* when you refer to Imelda's breasts. Does *sandías* mean breasts in Spanish?"

"No, of course not, Señor Thomas. If you ask a woman in Mexico for a *sandía* she will give you a watermelon. You must ask for her *tetas* if you want her titties. I was speaking figuratively. I think it's time for you to learn some Spanish, eh?"

"I don't want to learn Spanish and I think calling your wife's breasts watermelons is disrespectful."

"It is not disrespectful. Watermelons are large and sweet are they not? And Imelda's breasts, as you call them, are also large and sweet. Why else would you spend so much time observing them with such desire, Señor Thomas? Besides I do not think you should be telling me about treating my wife with respect, do you? But I shall not call them watermelons if doing so displeases you."

"Okay, okay, I see your point. Call them whatever you like. But tell me this, where did the little *bambino* come from? Certainly you haven't been on the road of thorns for a year. It all looks very suspicious to me, Arsenio."

"You are a very suspicious man, Señor Thomas, and that is not good for your health because a suspicious man never relaxes."

"Let me worry about my health, Arsenio. Are you going to tell me about the little *bambino* or not?"

"Of course I am, Señor Thomas, if that is what you wish but first if you are trying to practice your Spanish *bambino* is an Italian word, not a Spanish one. The Spanish word is *niño*."

"I am not trying to practice my Spanish. I was just wondering if the little whatever you want to call him is your son."

"See I was right about you not being able to relax. You are all excited and it is not unusual for a man your age to have a stroke or heart attack. I think that perhaps you should be with Imelda a little while to release some stress."

"Okay, Arsenio, forget about the kid. I shouldn't have asked. It's impossible to get a straight answer from you."

"The problem with you, Señor Thomas, is that you have little appreciation for the art of conversation. But for you I will answer your question about my son directly. It's true that the baby is not my biological son but I love him as if he were my own and shall raise him as my son."

"Whose son is he, then?"

"He is the son of Imelda's second husband."

"So when she ran off with you she took all three of his children. Is that it?"

"Señor Thomas, as you know, it is not good to separate a mother from her children. Even if she is a whore her children need her to do what a man should not have to do."

"Like changing their diapers."

"Exactly. You see, Señor Thomas, you and I agree on many things because we are both men."

"Finish your story, Arsenio." Just then Arsenio looks past me toward the kitchen.

"Señor Thomas, I believe your wife wishes to tell you something." I turn to find Anne standing quietly. I wonder how much of the conversation she has heard. She looks as if she's about to faint. I go to her and hold her. She doesn't resist or respond.

"What is it Anne? Were you able to get through to an operator?"

"No. I'm so tired, Jeffrey. I've dialed 911 a dozen times and each time I wait to speak to someone but no one answers just that damn recording."

"Señor Thomas, why is your wife dialing 911? Is there an emergency? Because if there is I may be able to help. Is it an illness?"

"It is *you*, all of you," Anne says almost in tears, "when are you going to leave our home?" she asks in a desperate tone of voice.

"Señora Thomas, that is none of your business. You should go back to the kitchen where you belong. Your husband and I are talking."

"You asshole *get the fuck out of my house!*" Anne screams with surprising energy.

"Señor Thomas, you have no control over your wife. Such a wife is an embarrassment."

"Arsenio, you are not helping matters. Anne, go back and try 911 again and I will see what Arsenio and I can work out."

"Work out? You fucking spineless idiot. Work out! Fuck you!" With that she storms back into the kitchen.

"Arsenio, you can see the problem your being here is causing, can't you?"

"No, the problem is that you cannot control your wife. She thinks she is a man but she is only a woman and such conversations are not for her. You do not hear Imelda saying such things." I turn to Imelda who has apparently grown tired of holding up her breasts to me though she continues to smile sweetly.

Turning back to Arsenio, I say, "Just finish your story, Arsenio, so we can discuss your leaving."

"Let's not talk about leaving. It's too unpleasant but I will finish my story. When I returned to my village many people came to greet me. So many old faces brought tears to my eyes and many, many young faces that I did not know, the children of my old friends, and very many cousins. They all were very happy to see me. You see I was a very important *Mexicano* to them because I had escaped to *Mexico Norte* in the U.S. and they all were very eager to hear my stories, especially the young men and women who plan every day for the long journey of thorns to paradise.

"And so I told them my stories and as I did they brought me many *cervezas*. Even the *policías* and *narcotraficantes* came to hear my stories. At first I was a little nervous when they arrived. They all have guns and it is not like in the U.S. where the police and criminals fear the courts. No, if they had wanted to rob and kill me they could have done so and nobody would have asked questions, not if they knew what was good for them. But like you, Señor Thomas, I am not stupid. I told them that if they ever came to Los Angeles they should come to see me, that I know people who can give them papers that will make them citizens. Such men as these would most likely know these people anyway but they too are very smart men who do not kill the chicken to get the egg. We Mexicans may fight with each other in Mexico but in the U.S. we know we must stick together.

"So I told them my stories and of course I told them only the stories about how very good it is to live in the U.S. because I did not want to discourage them because for many their only hope is the *journey to paradise* as the journey north to the America is often called.

"There were also many *niñōs* sitting on the floor listening to my stories and I did not wish to discourage them either. I told them that there were plenty of toys in America that would speak Spanish to them like Dora's Talking Kitchen, LeapFrog, and Elmo, who will sing *Dia Soleado* to them. And when one said that he would not be able to watch TV in America because he would understand nothing I told him not to worry because he would be able to watch TV shows for Hispanics like *Freddie* and *Go, Diego, Go* and that each year there are more and more Latino shows on TV because Hollywood knows that *Gringolándia* is quickly becoming *Latinolándia* so now all the movie makers love the Latino people and love to make movies for them. They even make fun of the old gringo movies by making movies about gay cowboys or about Jesus getting Mary Magdalene pregnant and living happily ever after. That is why many gringos watch only the old movies, like *Gone with the Wind, Stagecoach, The Grapes of Wrath, Casablanca,* and *On the Waterfront,* movies about an America that no longer exists for the gringos.

"But then one of the *narcotraficantes* said that the people in Hollywood do not love Latinos but love only their *dinero*. Of course I agreed saying it is understood that in America the dollar is God, but that, I said, is very good for us. And the same man, a very scary man, asked why is it good for us. And I told him in a way that he would understand. I agreed that the Americans who buy our drugs do not like us but as long as they have the money to make us rich what do we care? And that it is because the dollar is God in America that the American money worshipers who make us rich will continue to welcome us and our drugs and cheap labor and will make us feel at home with movies like *Spanglish* and *A Day without a Mexican* and with toys that speak Spanish to our children. And having heard what I said the man nodded in agreement and bought a round of drinks for everyone in my honor. I was relieved that he like what I said. Still it is impossible to be relaxed around such men. Like the weather they are unpredictable.

"So I continued, cheerfully explaining that the journey north will not take them to a strange land but to a Latino paradise, a *Nuevo Mexico* that their brothers and sisters are presently preparing for them. I told them that their arrival in the U.S. will not be a departing but a homecoming because their *compatriotas* will welcome them with open arms and tears in their eyes.

"And then with much love in my heart and with great solemnity I beseeched them to come. Like the Jews who returned to Palestine to reclaim their old homeland, the one given to them by God, I told them it was their duty as Mexicans to make the journey northward and join their brothers and sisters in their struggle to reclaim the promised land that was once theirs, not to take it by force, as the Jews did, but by occupation, not in anger, but with love in their hearts.

"'Your brothers and sisters,' I said to them, 'grow stronger each and every day, but still depend on those who follow if victory is to be achieved. Is that not why they send you the money they have worked so hard for, so that you can take the road northward? Mexico is the heart and lungs of the *Nuevo Mexico* that grows north of the border and you are the fresh blood that is the source of its increasing strength and vitality. Because of you, each day the *Americanos* grow weaker as we grow stronger and I believe that one day soon the two Mexicos will be reunited.'"

"Come on, Arsenio," I interject, "the land isn't yours. You speak the language of the people who stole it from the Indians. At least be honest. You are only stealing back what your Spanish-speaking ancestors stole in the first place."

"You are a very savvy gringo, Señor Thomas, so you know how the game is played. And like the Spanish your people used the Bible to justify the theft of the Indians' lands. Just now I spoke of the Jews returning to their homeland which their ancestors stole from the Canaanites and justified the theft by saying that Yahweh had given them the land because the Canaanites worshipped the wrong gods, gods that were vile, degrading, and immoral, which of course has nothing to do with one's right to the property one owns but is only an excuse for stealing that which belonged to another.

"And so today the Jews say they have the right to Palestine, which belonged to the Palestinians because long ago Yahweh allowed Joshua to steal the land of the Canaanites and to divide it among the Jews. You see how convenient this reasoning is, Señor Thomas. The word of God is as invisible as God himself so cannot be questioned. And so we are all thieves but at least my people are taking back what once belong to them, which is based on historical fact, not on the words of an invisible God. And though I speak the language of my people's conquerors, the blood of the native peoples who first lived upon the land before the arrival of the Europeans flows through my veins. Can you say the same, Señor Thomas?"

"No, I can't," I say, begrudgingly recognizing that Arsenio is, as he would say, not so stupid. Wearily I tell him to go on with his story.

"Yes, I will but you must be patient, Señor Thomas. As I have said you gringos are too impatient. I believe the world is in such bad shape because the white man has never been satisfied, always impatient so never appreciating what he already has. I must tell you, Señor Thomas, that the poor Mexicans living in poor villages are happier than you gringos with your SUVs and big houses and lonely neighborhoods."

As if in a hypnotic state I listen to him, my eyes occasionally glancing toward Imelda. Ignoring his remarks about the gringos, since I pretty much agree with him, I say, "Didn't the Canaanites use prostitutes in their religion?" hating myself afterwards for introducing yet another digression.

"You see, you are an educated man, Señor Thomas. Yes they used prostitutes because they worshipped the elements of nature. Imelda would have been a priestess. Unlike the Jews and Christians, the Canaanites worshipped the forces of life not death, not a dead man hanging on a cross."

"Jesus! Arsenio," I exclaim shocked by his lack of respect toward the Crucifixion but also thinking that Imelda probably would have been considered an epiphany of a goddess.

"Exactly, Señor Thomas. Of course the Canaanites' religion was considered degrading because it was full of violence and corruption but tell me what is more violent and corrupt than the destruction of cities?"

I say nothing, knowing Arsenio would answer the question himself. Like his wife I had fallen under the spell of this Pancho Villa look-alike.

"So the Jews stole the territories of the Canaanites because their God had handed the cities over to them. You see. in their eyes it wasn't theft but the receiving of a divine gift. And the first of the Canaanite cities to be destroyed was Jericho and it is said that *'they devoted to destruction by the edge of the sword all in the city, both men and women, young and old, oxen, sheep, and donkeys.'* But of course they saved one prostitute and her family so that they would afterwards feel no guilt and believe that they were a good people. Then they continued to the city of Ai and destroyed it. And afterward destroyed many other cities until the land of the Canaanites was divided among the tribes of the Jews. And do you know what the name of Canaan is today?"

"Palestine," I say wearily.

"Yes, so you see, Señor Thomas, that it was the Jews, whose religion your people inherited, who legitimized the game of taking other peoples' land in the name of God and taking it back as one's homeland if it is lost temporarily. Your people stole the homelands of the Indians, who stole them from no one, and the homelands of the Mexicans, whose conquerors the Spanish had stolen from the Indians, our true ancestors. And now like the Jews we seek the return of our homelands. You do not like it but that is the way the game is played and the game book is the same for the gringos as it is for the Mexicans—the Bible.

"That's just great, Arsenio. I'm happy to know that your people will beat us at our own game and soon conquer us. So is your little story finished?"

"You are bitter, Señor Thomas, but should not be. Think of the benefits to you and your people. Have you not enjoyed gazing upon Imelda's *sandías* has given you?" I resist looking at Imelda, fearing that doing so will validate Arsenio's point.

"Get on with it, Arsenio. You may have all day but I don't. Furthermore, you and your family have kept Anne and me from our jobs and there is no way we're going back to them with all of you in our house. No way! And that's why you must go. Today!"

"See, Señor Thomas, what did I just tell you? You gringos are always in such a big hurry—rush, rush, rush—and don't take the time to live. The day is yet young. As I said before, you could learn a great deal from the Mexican people. You make fun of us, saying we are the *mañana* people but what you do not see is that we know how to live for today. And politically your impatience has been a disaster. Isn't that why you are in a stupid and costly war, because your *presidente* was in a big hurry? You will not conquer Iraq. But look at the Latino people. We are in no hurry. A few of us come each and every day like the rain that gives life to the earth."

"A *few*? I'd say more like a flood that sweeps away everything, like the hurricanes in New Orleans."

"Perhaps, Señor Thomas, a stream from a great lake."

"More like a river flowing out of the ocean."

"You are either very ignorant or very funny, Señor Thomas. You must know that rivers flow to the ocean not from it."

"We're not talking about water, Arsenio, but people, and south of the border are three oceans flooding into America—Mexico, Central America, and South America—and compared to your half billion, which will soon be a billion people, we anglos are nothing. Oh to hell with all this water talk. What's your point, Arsenio?"

"Yes, let's not talk about water. There will be plenty of time in the future for water talk, when the oceans, as you say, flow onto the land, but that will be a topic for our children to discuss. What I wanted to say is very serious, that your *presidente* will not conquer Iraq but we Latinos will conquer America because we come with open hands and smiles on our faces," and as he said this he grinned broadly and held out the palms of his hands.

"Arsenio, I don't need you to lecture me on how stupid my *presidente* is. I knew that long before you arrived. So skip the politics." *Why am I standing here talking to this man?*

"I see talk of politics depresses you and I understand. We Mexicans know something about corrupt politics. That is why we flee Mexico, because it is a sinking ship of corruption. And what do our politicians do? They do what all politicians do. They become rich. We are not so different you and I, Señor Thomas, but I did not mean to talk of bad things but of the importance of living for today and letting *mañana* take care of itself. To speak frankly, I do not think the future is ours to control. It never has been. It is true that I live to serve my people and their future but I think what will happen will happen anyway.

"You gringos complain about the millions of illegal immigrants entering the U.S. but it could not have been otherwise. When water is added to a glass that is already full the water overflows the glass and goes elsewhere. It cannot do otherwise. It is a law of nature. So why worry about tomorrow? Is it not better to live in the moment?

"Gazing at Imelda's *sandías* were you not able to get off the trouble train of time and breathe the fresh air and enjoy the trees and flowers and the sky and sun, so to speak."

"Stop it, Arsenio! This is my home not Tahiti and I'm tired and don't want to hear any more about Imelda's *sandías*, as you continue to call your wife's breasts."

"No doubt you are tired. I understand..."

No, apparently you do not understand, Arsenio. Just get on with your story or I'm going into the kitchen and dial 911 myself."

"No, I don't wish that you leave just now. Maybe later but now, as you say, I must finish my story. Besides I don't think 911 works. At least it doesn't in L.A. I will explain but I must tell you little story in order to do this."

"Oh God! Arsenio, you haven't even finished the one you're telling me."

"You are exhausted, Señor Thomas, and should sit down next to Imelda and rest yourself."

"Thanks, Arsenio, but I'll stand. So tell me the little story but be quick about it... and don't say a word about my impatience. You would be impatient too if you were me."

"You are so funny, Señor Thomas. I really enjoy talking to you. Well the story begins one day when my family and I were gathered in front of the TV. We were yelling exuberantly and waving Mexican flags because the Mexican soccer team was beating the Americans, who are not as you know very good at soccer, but that is not so important. The Americans are good at other sports like baseball though I think that perhaps the Cubans, Puerto Ricans, and Dominicans are not so bad either. And your basketball and football teams would be nothing were it not for the black athletes. Even in golf the superstar Tiger Woods looks more like me than you. Soon the only gringos in sports will be the spectators. Ha ha ha... Don't look so serious, Señor Thomas. I'm only kidding a little."

"Damn it, Arsenio, can't you stick to one topic?"

"Don't be angry, Señor Thomas. How can we ever be friends if you are always getting angry?"

"We'll *never, ever* be friends, Arsenio. Get on with the fucking story."

"Such language is not good, especially in front of the children, but I will ignore it, Señor Thomas. And if we shall never be friends it won't be because I haven't made an effort. But what I wanted to say is that life is very complex and each story consists of many smaller stories but I will do my best stick to one story since I can see that you are becoming easily irritated. You know, Señor Thomas, I am surprised that a man who teaches stories would be so impatient with them?"

"How do you know I am a teacher, Arsenio?"

"Let's not get distracted by such a small detail. Allow me to return to my little story about 911. So my family and I are all together watching the TV when suddenly we are disturbed by the sound of gunshots. Immediately we all drop to the floor so as not to be hit by a stray bullet. The poor people in Iraq must live their lives on the floor.

"Anyway after the shooting stops we get up and I look out the window. What do I see? A boy, a teenager, lying on the sidewalk. No one else is outside because they are afraid the shooters will return but after a few minutes people start to come out of their houses and approach the body. I tell my family to stay inside but of course the boys, excited to see the body, run outside before I can stop them.

"The man's eyes are a little open but they do not blink, so I think he is dead but I am not sure he cannot be helped by the doctors at the emergency room because they are very good doctors with much sophisticated equipment. I know this because my wife went to the emergency room to have all our children and many times we've had to use the emergency room because we have no medical insurance or a regular doctor. And if they call the immigration authorities they know they will be in big trouble because their job, you might say, is to heal not squeal. By now there are many cell phones out but I see they are being used to take pictures of the body to be displayed on the Internet, which is a very popular thing to do in Mexico. I ask if someone has called 911 but no one responds. I know they haven't because they are afraid of the police even more than they are afraid of the drive-by shooters. I too do not call because I am not legal either, though I've been in the U.S. for many years. I see that the body has many bullet holes and I watch the man's blood drain off the sidewalk into the brown grass. I think that even if the man is alive now he will soon be dead."

"What's this got to do with 911? If no one calls then of course it won't work."

"That is true and I am coming to that, Señor Thomas, if you will not interrupt.

"Jesus!" I exclaim.

"You must be a very religious man, Señor Thomas."

"It's an expression, Arsenio, a way of expressing my frustration. If there were a God in heaven he would have answered my wife's prayers and you would no longer be here."

"That is a cruel thing to say but I will ignore it because I know you are disturbed so I shall finish my story. After a time the family of the boy who has been shot arrives and the mother kneels down by boy and pulls him to her and then begins to cry. A young woman, I think the boy's sister, takes out her cell phone and dials 911. It is the right thing to do. You cannot leave a body of a human being on the sidewalk like it was a cat or dog or in the water as your government did in New Orleans. It's not right. And it is not good for children to see such things because then they think that society doesn't care about people. What could be more frightening to a child or to adults for that matter? So someone always calls. But the police do not come. No one comes until the body is cold and has been covered by a blanket provided by a good Samaritan, most likely one of the women who are weeping for the dead man."

"Was he a boy or a man, Arsenio? You can't seem to make up your mind."

"They think they are men until they are shot and lie dead on the ground. Then you see they are only boys."

"You're depressing me, Arsenio. I don't think I can take this much longer."

"You should not be depressed, Señor Thomas. You have a beautiful house, a beautiful wife, and you are an American citizen. You carry no green card. You do not have to fear the authorities. And besides you've been enjoying looking at Imelda's beautiful titties though perhaps I think you may have done more than just look but that is not important. And I also think you have enjoyed at least a little discussing religion and politics with me, who wishes to be your friend though you do not wish to be my friend. Believe me you have no reason to be depressed, Señor Thomas."

"I have five reasons to be depressed, Arsenio, and they're all sitting in my living room, six if I count the baby. And I would appreciate it if you would not say any more about your wife's breasts."

"I understand, Señor Thomas. You wish to get them out of your mind and are having trouble doing so. You are a good man and for you I will return to my story."

"Your story? You mean you're not finished?"

"I finished only the little story. You must sit down, Señor Thomas. You've been standing there a very long time and you are very fatigued after last night. Sit down, there, next to Imelda. She would love to have you next to her. I think she likes you very much and though she is my first wife and mother of my firstborn I will not be jealous. And I know Lope will not mind either because he has gotten all his anger out. He is no longer angry at you, not now." I look at Lope and to me his expression seems quite grim.

"He looks angry."

"Of course he looks angry. He sees you staring at his mother's breasts and then ungratefully demand that we should leave. And he hears us calling his mother a whore. But he doesn't understand that those things do not matter. It was natural that she would become a whore and even more so that she would show her gratitude to you by allowing you to look upon her beautiful *titties*. And I am sure she would allow you suck on them if you wished because she knows you are unhappy and when a man is unhappy he becomes a baby and needs a tit to suck on. And don't feel ashamed. You gringos are too uptight about such things.

"Think of those poor men who have no titties available to them. You know the men I speak of, they who sit in bars, alone and unhappy. They are like babies who want their mother's tit but instead have a bottle with a rubber *tetilla* shoved into their mouth. That is the way with you gringos. Everything is so artificial. Mexican babies do not suck rubber *tetillas* but real *tetillas*. You are looking at me strangely, Señor Thomas. I know why. It is because you do not know this word either. *Tetilla* means a woman's tit. *Tetillas* is the plural form..."

"Spare me the grammar lesson, Arsenio, and that's not why I'm looking at you strangely. It's because I find all this talk about titties very unnecessary."

"Señor Thomas, I would think that you of all men would be interested in what I have to say about a woman's titties."

"Okay, I deserve that, Señor Freud. Finish what you have to say."

"I like your sense of humor, Señor Thomas, and as you know these days a sense of humor can be a man's best friend. Nevertheless I think Señor Freud would agree that you gringos are a little crazy and I think it is because your lives have become too artificial. That is why the Mexicans living in the United States will always be loyal to their mother Mexico, because she is truly a mother not a machine. But you are fortunate, Señor Thomas. You have Imelda's *tetillas* to suck on if you desire as well as the little *naranjas* of your beautiful wife..."

"Leave my wife out of the conversation, Arsenio." I didn't know what the word meant and didn't dare ask. But watching and listening to Arsenio I begin to get a very creepy feeling about him, that there is much more to the man than I first understood.

"That's very unfair of you, Señor Thomas. Here you enjoy the flesh of my first wife and Lope's mother but become angry because I speak of your wife's *naranjas.* That is so unfair, so like you gringos. However, because we are friends..."

"Arsenio, we *are not* friends. And I have not enjoyed the flesh of your wife."

"Perhaps only in the way President Carter speaks of but have you ever told Imelda to cover herself?"

"No. It's not my place to tell a nursing woman to cover her breasts."

"Yes, I understand. And I know you only make a joke about our not being friends but if it makes you happy I cannot be angry. And just to please you I will not refer to your beautiful wife's *naranjas.* But as I said, Señor Thomas, you are exhausted and should rest a little. Please sit next to Imelda. Look, I think she is in love with you and I do not mind. And do not worry about Lope. He must learn the ways of the world. That women are meant to be whores for men because no man can live with one woman. That is why I take Imelda back to L.A. with me so I can live like your Mormons who have many wives which is perfectly natural and my second wife will not complain because she will have another woman to help in the kitchen. Imelda is a wonderful cook. Perhaps she should stay a while with you to help your wife in the kitchen."

"I don't think that would be a good idea, Arsenio. Apparently you haven't been paying attention to my wife's feelings toward all of you—especially Imelda."

"Your wife does seem to be a very jealous woman."

"It's not jealousy. If Imelda were to stay here you'd have a reason to visit and one visit from you is enough."

"You are so funny, Señor Thomas, a very funny man. But sit down before you fall down."

He's right. I am beginning to feel as if I'm about to faint but the only places to sit are next to Imelda or Lope so I walk over to Imelda who smiles graciously and pulls at her nipples. I wedge myself between her and the arm of the sofa. I can feel her soft body next to me and she turns slightly so that one of her breasts touches my arm. I pull away but to no avail. I look at Lope who stares back with a hate in his eyes. I hate him and I hate his father, if Arsenio is his father. *What is wrong with me that I'm so incapable of acting? It's as if the Arsenio's family is a clan of spiders and I've become caught in their web. Or I should say they have turned my home into a web and my family has become their prey*. Mostly I am just tired and find myself falling asleep. Then Anne walks into the room.

"Once again I see you have everything under control, Jeffrey." She's furious.

"I just needed to rest a little."

"Well you've certainly found a comfortable spot." Imelda has placed her head on my shoulder and her breasts have fallen toward me so that they almost lie in my lap.

"I must have dozed off. It's not what you think, Anne," I say as I try to push Imelda's breasts away from me. Imelda keeps her head on my shoulder and smiles sweetly. I try to remove Imelda's breast from my lap but with little success.

"You're right, Jeffrey, it's not what I think. It's far worse. When you are done there, I want to talk to you in the kitchen."

"It's not what you think, Anne. I'm coming..."

"You sick fuck," I hear Anne say from a distance and then the kitchen door slam against the wall.

"Move, Imelda. Now my wife is furious with me." I look a Lope, who is staring at me like a python. And then at Arsenio, who is smiling, almost laughing. I get up and Imelda says, "Señor Thomas, come back to your mama Imelda, come to your mama, Señor Thomas."

As I look about me in my trance-like state I can see the entire family calmly sitting and watching me as if they were sitting before a TV set. The two children look at me wide-eyed, their little mouths partly open. They have witnessed the transformation of an adult into an idiot, which, as Arsenio says, they are too young to fully understand. I stand there looking at them, feeling shame and disgust for my failure to act as a man and protect my family and home. Then I hear weeping. It's Anne standing by the kitchen door. She walks closer but does not enter the living room.

"What has happened to you, Jeffrey? Look at yourself. My God! You are as helpless as a baby." I look down and see that Imelda is holding my hand. What can I say? An apology seems inadequate.

"Is this your new family, Jeffrey? Have you forgotten your real family? I need your help. 911 doesn't respond but maybe you really don't care. Maybe you think having *them* here *is* okay. I am sure that *she* can give you what I could never give you. But look at the house. *Just Look!* And what about your daughter? What about *Kelly*? She is in the kitchen. She's been crying and is distraught but will not talk to me. Maybe I should bring her here to talk to you."

Though I know she would never do that just the idea sends shivers through me. "No, no. Don't you dare do that," I say. "I'm coming. Go! I'll be right there. Go on, *please!*" She turns and walks away.

Then I notice that Imelda is still holding my hand. *Jesus, there's no getting away from her!* I shake my hand loose. The mention of Kelly brings over me a wave of anxiety and anger. I realize I have been seduced and hoodwinked by Imelda."

"Señor Thomas, I can see Imelda likes you very much and since we are friends you may take her anytime you wish."

"Shut the fuck up, Arsenio!"

"Why are you angry—because your wife is angry? That is to be expected but it will pass. It always does. They love us then they hate us, but they will always love us again. That is the way it is with men and women."

I don't reply but briefly stare at Arsenio as if I were experiencing an epiphany. I realize now that his cunning borders on genius. I turn and walk toward the kitchen.

"Señor Thomas!" It's Imelda. I look back and see she hurries towards me.

"Damn it, Imelda, what is it?" I say, my exasperation becoming unbearable.

"You must calm yourself, Señor Thomas. Your wife does not understand us but you do."

"I understand you, all of you, very well." *God I hate them!* I wish I could turn into the fucking Terminator and slaughter them, even the two kids who are now wiggling their tongues at me like little demons.

"Goddamn it, Imelda, get away from me!"

"You don't like me anymore, Señor Thomas?"

"I never liked you, Imelda. I felt sorry for you but now I see my sympathy was a trap."

"No, you were acting as a good Christian for the Bible says, '*You shall also love the stranger, for you were strangers in the land of Egypt.*'"

"Fuck the Bible!"

"To say such a thing is a sin, Señor Thomas."

"No, my sin is my failure to protect my family."

"I know why you are unhappy with me. You think I am a whore don't you? We were happy before Arsenio came but now because of him you think I am a whore."

"I don't think you are a whore. I think you are a very cunning woman and ever since you arrived I have been very unhappy."

"Then you do not dislike Imelda, Señor Thomas?"

"Imelda, why did you leave a husband who loved you to come here with that monster Arsenio who calls you a whore? Where is he by the way? Arsenio didn't finish his story. And really why are his children here? And stop grabbing at my hand." Arsenio is chortling in the background and when I look up the others renew their demonic pantomime causing me to quickly return my attention to Imelda.

"Don't mind their foolishness, Señor Thomas. They are a bunch of donkeys. But since you speak of my second husband I will complete Arsenio's story. Arsenio came back to Mexico to take Lope with him to L.A. And when he announced this Lope was ready to go because he had seen many movies about the gangs in L.A. and thought they were very cool because they have beautiful cars that jump up and down like grasshoppers and beautiful women and best of all they have guns. The gangsters in Mexico are not so cool, not like the *cholos* in L.A. In Mexico they drive SUVs and wear cowboy boots and western hats and look like your Marlboro man whose cigarettes they smoke. So when Arsenio came, he and Lope went off for a long time and drank beer. Amancio, my second husband, did not mind because Lope was not his son and they never got along.

"I know what Arsenio told him because he and Lope have talked much about it since we left my village. At first Lope was full of questions about L.A. because like I said he had seen and heard much about the city on television. Arsenio told him that there were many great Latino cities in the U.S. but L.A. was the greatest Mexican city, Mexico City *al Norte* he called it.

"Then he smiled and said 'You know, Lope, L.A. is now called the Tamale Capital of the World, the very place where the International Tamale Festival is held. Not in Mexico City, not anywhere south of the gringo border but in L.A.'

"Lope smiled too and said 'You are joking me, Papa.'

"'I do not joke you, Lope, because it is the truth. But you are also correct because it is a joke played on the gringo by the Mexican people. And you and

I can laugh because in L.A. you will be welcome by your own people who will help you to become very successful.'

"Then Arsenio told Lope about the mayor Antonio Villaraigosa who is a very big hero in Mexico to begin to explain to him what he called *La Reconquista.*

"'Look at Villaraigosa' Arsenio said 'the mayor of L.A. He is the child of immigrants who were probably illegal like us. Like the great Latino *Generalisimo* César Chávez, who I know you know because all Mexicans know of César Chávez, and like the great *general* and *revolucionario* Rodolfo Gonzales, who you do not know but will one day, Villaraigosa, like those men, is a *nortemejicano*, not an *Americano*, a leader in the *El Movimiento.*'

"'*El Movimiento?*' asked Lope.

"'Yes, about which I have much to tell you but for now I will say to you only that it is the movement to reclaim the homelands the gringo stole from the Mexican people, *La Reconquista*, and that is what is happening today and Villaraigosa is one of its leaders and L.A. is one of its victories. He calls L.A. *the Venice of the 21st century* but we all know that he means *the Mexico City al Norte of the 21st century.* When he was younger Villaraigosa demanded Mexican American studies in high school and fought for Chicano rights in college. And now he leads a Latino city, where seventy-one percent school children are Latino, and their numbers shall increase as the gringo children continue to flee to the suburbs. In the schools you see the future of the city and when you are my age, Lope, I believe the gringo children will be at most five percent and these will be the children of the very rich gringos who live in gated communities, like the fortified Green Zone in Baghdad, and send their children to very expensive private school that will have plenty of security like those for the wealthy in Mexico.'

"'And the gringos who cannot not afford to live in such communities, where will they go, Papa?'

"'I do not know, my son, nor do I care. Perhaps to Iowa or South Dakota where there are fewer Mexicans. But our people go to those places as well to work the fields and in the meat processing factories...'"

"But papa why are gringos unwilling to work in the fields and in those factories?"

"The gringo thinks such work is below him. But that will be the secret of our success. The jobs gringos do not like to do are the ones that require many people. I will give you an example. The city of El Centro, California, is in a big farming area and most the jobs are farming jobs. Who is going to do the work? Mexicans of course. And Mexicans work in all the other businesses as well, even for the Border Patrol because Spanish is the dominant language. So what do the gringo children do? The ones who parents are not owners of farms or big businesses leave. They don't like the work or the hot weather. But we Mexicans flourish wherever there is work and the weather is not so comfortable. So today the City of El Centro is a Mexican city with very few gringos. And that is what will happen in places like Iowa and North Dakota. So perhaps one day there will be no place for the gringos to go except Canada. Ha ha ha... The gringo is very funny. You know *la migra* has a big office in the city of El Centro because Imperial County borders Mexico. But I think they are not very good at their job. If they were, El Centro would not be a Mexican city. And it is strange that the city is full of illegal aliens but no one checks to see if they are in the country illegally because it is against the law to do so. An illegal gets caught only if he gets caught breaking a different law like driving too fast. And even then he can get an immigration lawyer to help him or go back to Mexico for a week and then return to the U.S. as I have just done. But that is why it is smart not to get caught breaking any America laws even little one like running a red light. If you break a big one you will go to prison though you will find many of your amigos there as well. We Mexicans are to be found everywhere in America."

"Because gringos are very stupid."

"Which is very good for us. But let me tell you a little more about Villaraigosa and how he is a good example of how the gringo is his own worst enemy. When Villaraigosa was sick gringos healed him, when he was a thug they forgave him, and later when he had illegitimate children and was charged with assault and battery, none of that mattered. He was welcome at UCLA, one of America's finest universities, because he was Latino, and there he became an important *soldado* in the Chicano Movement. And now he is the mayor of America's greatest city and even Governor Arnold Schwarzenegger caters to him because he knows that he will be finished as governor without the Latino vote. And when Villaraigosa speaks to the people about *Presidente* Bush's State of the Union address he does so in Spanish. Who knows, when you are my age, Mayor Antonio Villaraigosa may be *Presidente* Antonio Villaraigosa making the State of the Union address in Spanish; then the state of the union will be Hispanic and *The Star-Spangled Banner* will be sung in

Spanish. No, doubt, Lope, you have already heard this version song even in the village,'

"'Yes, Papa. Everyone in Mexico has heard it on the radio. It makes them very happy because they laugh a lot when they hear it but from what you say it is not just a joke but a sign of change.'

"'You are very wise to see that, Lope, unlike the unwise gringos who are mostly blind. Yes, the new song is both a joke and a portent and it should make the people of the village happy because it is the *nortemejicanos'* welcoming song to their brothers and sisters south of the border. And yes, it is also a joke because in America we Latinos call the song *The Star-Spanglish Banner.*

"'And the gringos, what do they think of their song's new name?'

"'They do not like it, of course. No one likes a joke when it is about himself. But we have every reason to be happy. I just spoke of Mayor Antonio Villaraigosa yet he has not been alone in the struggle to recapture L.A. for the Mexican people. There are now hundreds of Latino politicos in office in L.A. but I shall speak only of the greatest, such as the late *grande general* of L.A.'s Latino Workers Army that is now over a million strong, Miguel Contreras, whose parents, like us, traveled *el camino de espinas al norte* to join the struggle of their brothers and sisters in the U.S. Of course to the gringo union members Contreras is not a hero, but *un enemigo.* That is because they can read the graffiti on the wall that says **The gringo is history in L.A**. They saw it in the revolutionary red T-shirts worn by Contreras's followers, shirts that said *Unite Here,* but not even they understood the true meaning of the words which is *Soldados Unidos por El Movimiento.* He was a good man who knew what I know and what you will now know, that roughly one-quarter of Mexico's work force is employed in *Mexico Norte USA.'*

"Arsenio shook his head and laughed a little laugh, as he often does when telling Lope about America and about you gringos. But then he continued about the great Miguel Contreras."

"'Contreras was *un gran general* who devoted his life to the people—*the Latino people.* And who followed behind his casket during his magnificent funeral? Yes, the great Villaraigosa with his arm around the son of *el general.* *Un soldado* had fallen but other heroes follow, an army remains, *la guerra* continues.

"'The gringo is truly *loco*. Who else would welcome the thief into his home, feed him, care for his health, educate him, and then forgive him when he steals his home and drives his family into the street? That is what has happened in L.A. But of course Mexicans did not really steal L.A. from the gringos. They only took back what had been first stolen from them.'

"Arsenio then explained that when we got to L.A. he would first introduce Lope to important people in the *Mexican Militia* who would take care of him. He explained that to gringos Latino gangsters are just criminals, but to the *Mexicanos* they are *soldados* fighting for *nuestra raza*, our people the Mexican people, like the Iraqi *insurgencia* who fight a *jihad* against the U.S. infidels who invaded their spiritual homeland as they had invaded the spiritual homeland of the Indians.

"Arsenio is a little bit right when he says you gringos are stupid because you don't know what is happening. He told Lope that when we get to America that we would see many cars with bumper stickers that say *Jo* ♥ *Aztlán* but the gringo, he said is too stupid to know what it means. I felt a little stupid myself because I did not know either. Then Arsenio explained to Lope that *we* are the people of Aztlán, the Chicano people, who come seeking new homes in the old lands that once belonged to our people. He then explained that César Chávez is the Latinos' peaceful Patton, so called after your famous general, and that Chávez was a humble man, like Jesus who spoke of peace but thought of war. Arsenio told him what Jesus said: "*Do not think that I have come to bring peace to the earth. I have not come to bring peace, but a sword.*'

"Arsenio said that Jesus also told the people that he came to bring division, not peace, saying, 'From now on in one house there will be five divided, three against two and two against three.' Lope did not understand about the house nor did I. So Arsenio explained that to the Mexican people that house is America. And that today we are the two in the house but soon will be three then four. But most important the American house will remain divided. He explained that the gringo wants to melt the Mexicans in the American melting pot but that we will not be melted because we are the *carne* that refuses to be melted, unlike the gringos who have become soft like stewed *frijoles*.

"He said that there are many great generals leading the Chicano people in Aztlán but that he believes César Chávez was the greatest because he truly outsmarted the stupid gringos. Forgive me, Señor Thomas, but those were his words, and I know you want me to speak truthfully to you. He said you

Americanos are too stupid to see that like Julius Caesar, whose name he bears, César Chávez was not a man of peace but a conqueror, and like the Romans, whose language we speak, we too come to conquer. *'Veni, vidi, vici''*—those are the words of the Roman Caesar. And now ours are the same. Each morning Arsenio would begin the day by saying, *'Nosotros venimos, vemos, vencemos.'*

"One night Arsenio asked Lope if he knew the symbol of the eagle on the Mexican flag and Lope said *of course*. And Arsenio said that was very good, but explained that today the symbol has a different meaning. He said that as always the eagle remains a symbol of the Mexican people but now the serpent in its claw and beak is the gringo people and that the cactus it is perched on is the culture of the Mexican people and that the rock it grows from is Aztlán, the Mexican homeland stolen by the gringos. For Lope this was very new and hard to understand and so he asked his father what it all means and to this Arsenio smiled and said 'It means, Lope, that the Mexicans will conquer the gringo and return the Mexican culture to its ancient homeland.'

"One evening Arsenio became very serious and spoke to Lope in the manner of a priest who speaks of an important matter to his *acólitado* and I remember this discussion very well because I too liked what Arsenio said about my people. He began by telling Lope that in order to truly appreciate *El Movimiento* he must first understand *la vista grande de la vida*, the big picture of life. Then Arsenio asked Lope if he had ever heard of Charles Darwin but Lope hadn't. Neither had I. He said that Darwin explained how life is a struggle for survival, that only the strong survive, not the weak, but that the strong do not have to be big like the dinosaurs who no longer exist, but only tough. Then he explained that the strongest species of all time is very small, the cockroach. Lope said that he believed it because they were in every house of the village. And Arsenio said that's right and asked 'What happens when a new house is built?'

"'The cockroaches invade it,' Lope said 'and afterwards they cannot be driven away.'

"'Yes, exactly,' said Arsenio.

"Then Arsenio explained that we Mexicans are the cockroach people. 'You did not know this, Lope, but it is true and has been known for a long time. To the gringo such an idea would be insulting but we understand that the cockroach is greater than the dinosaur and that it is an honor to be a cockroach. We are *la gente cucaracha* and we travel *el camino de espinas al norte* so that only the toughest cockroaches reach the U.S. to resettle in the big houses the dinosaur gringos built on the land that was once ours and once we are there we will not go away again. We will be there forever like the cockroaches that are everywhere forever.'

"'But they will try to kill us, to trap us,' said Lope, 'just as the people try to kill the cockroaches that invade their houses.'

"'That is true, Lope,' said Arsenio, 'but they will capture and kill only a few and when their houses are filled with very many cockroaches they will leave.'

"'And so we are the *gent cucaracha* invading the big American house of the gringos,' said Lope. 'Still it does seem insulting to be compared to cockroaches, like something the gringos would say about us.'

"'Gringos would not have been smart enough to call us the cockroach people and I will tell you why, Lope.'

"And after he said that, Arsenio smiled a very sly smile as he often does, so Lope and I were very interested. But Arsenio said nothing for a moment to create little suspense in us and finally Lope said 'Yes, Papa, please tell us.'

"'I will tell you but I waited just a little so that you think carefully on what I am about to say. The idea that we are like cockroaches is too frightening for the gringo to face. It is a nightmare for him, a nightmare that he forgets when he awakes but of course it does not go away when he awakes. Do you understand, Lope?'

"'Yes, Papa, I think I do.'

"'Then can you tell me why it is a nightmare, an idea that the gringos do not want to think upon?'

"'Because cockroaches are everywhere, I think.'

"'That is good but there is more. Did the house where you lived before I came to claim you as my son, did it have cockroaches?'

"'Yes of course. All the houses in the world I believe have them.'

"'That is correct but did you and your mother not try to exterminate them?'

"'Yes, many times . . . . Ah, now I see what you mean. Once in the house the cockroach cannot be defeated. That is what the gringo cannot face.'

"'Yes,' said Arsenio. 'Everyone knows that but the gringo and that is our power over him. He will wait too long. In fact he has already waited too long. In America we now fill the cities; cultivate and harvest fields; work in factories; load and unload ships and planes; clean rooms in motels and hotels, office buildings, stores, and restaurants; prepare food and sell merchandise in a hundred thousand businesses; manicure lawns and gardens; baby-sit gringo *ninõs*; care for their sick in hospitals and the their elderly in nursing homes; and soon we shall be below the earth digging their coal, our faces black and proud. Yes, Lope, we are like the cockroach who is always busy and everywhere, visible and invisible. So you can see that it is an honor to be associated with the cockroach, who defeated the dinosaur in the race of time. And of all the people of the world only a Mexican would have the wisdom know this.'

"'You, Papa?' asked Lope proudly.

"'No, Lope, it was not my idea,' said Arsenio, and I could see that Lope was a little disappointed.

"'You are a good son to think so but your father is not so wise.'

"'Yes, of course you are. You are very wise, Papa.' I could see that what Lope had said made Arsenio very happy.

"'Lope, it is good that we are together because now my life is complete, but I will tell you that yes it is true that your father knows many things and perhaps is wise in some but it is the wisdom of our people not my own. Your father is only *un soldado en El Movimiento*, not a general, and my wisdom is to pay attention to those of our people who are truly wise, unlike the gringos who listen only to foolishness.

"'The *hombre* I now speak of was *un gran soldado y un teórico en El Movimiento*. His name is Oscar Zeta Acosta and was known as the Robin Hood Chicano lawyer. He wrote a book called *The Revolt of the Cockroach People*. When I first came to the U.S. I knew very little English so I went to a bookstore in L.A. called *Librería Nestore* that sells Spanish language books because I was too shy to go to a gringo bookstore. At the counter stood the store's owner, a bearded old blue-eyed Mexican who looked very strange to me. I thought he might be a gringo but could detect no gringo accent when we spoke. His name was Nestore Lopez and he welcomed me warmly.

"'I told him I wanted to learn English. He talked with me a little while and before I knew it I was telling him of my journey from Mexico. He then advised me not to talk about such things to strangers not even if they are

Mexican. He told me to watch gringo television and to read English wherever I went, when on the street to read the gringo signs and when in a store to read labels, and so on, and to speak English whenever possible. Of course he said for this I would have to sometimes leave the barrios of L.A. which are in truth Mexican towns. Then he explained that Spanish is the language of my people but that English is the language of success. "Keep the one in your heart and the other in your hand" he said.

"'Then he went to the back of the store and returned with the book that I speak of *The Revolt of the Cockroach People* and a small bilingual dictionary. "Keep the dictionary with you always," he said. "When you see an English word you do not know look it up and say it in the way the dictionary tells you." Then he told me that if I had any questions about what I read to come and see him and he would answer my questions.

"'I came back many times and read many of his books which he helped me to choose. He was the man who taught me English but he also taught me many things about the Mexican people. At first I wanted only to know about him but he would only smile and shake his old head a little. Once he said "Arsenio, I am not important. It is our people who are important. It is our people who have given importance to my life. When I came to America I came only to be part of the struggle to reclaim our homeland. I did not come for the reason that so many Mexicans come to America, for a job. I came for *la patria*."

"'Eventually I learned that Señor Lopez came from a small village south of Mexico City where they still speak Nahuatl, the mother tongue of our people.'

"'Papa, I thought Spanish was our language.'

"'Before I met this man I did not know so many things. It was from Señor Lopez that I learned that Spanish is the language of the conquerors of our people, not the mother tongue of our people, though now we have made it our own. He warned that the Mexican people must be careful to preserve their language which he called the spiritual matrix, the womb or parent of our culture. He believed that our people had already separated themselves from the deepest roots of their culture when they adopted the language and religion of their conquerors. And now they are learning a newer language even more remote from what he said the Greeks would call the *archê* of their culture.'

"'That is a very strange word, Papa. What does it mean?'

"'You are right, my son, it is a very strange word and I will tell you what Señor Lopez said it means. He said that every culture has its source like the wellspring of a stream and it consists of the basic principles of a culture. He said the land on which people live, the history of the people, and their traditions, rituals, and ceremonies are all part of their culture's *archê*, but most basic of all is a people's language. He said that is why the European invaders of our land forced the indigenous people to learn the language of the Europeans and to forget their *lengua materna*. And he said that when a people surrender their mother language they surrender their souls.

"'*That* is why the Mexican people have demanded Spanish be taught in the schools so that the Mexican children do not become separated from the soul of their culture and become lost as the gringo is lost. That is what Señor Lopez, this man of books, told me and I could see that he was very serious about the importance of language.'

"'But, Papa, is not English the language of the gringos? So why are they lost if they speak their language? I do not understand.'

"'That is a very intelligent question, Lope, the very one I asked Señor Lopez and he told me that English is a bastard language that has no soul. He said that it is a remarkable language because it can say anything but that it is dead because it grew without roots, stealing its words from languages that were rooted in the lives of peoples whose ways were rooted in the ways of the Earth. It is he said the language of the modern world like an operating language of a computer and nothing more. Then he said a very strange thing—that English was more dead than the ancient languages which are no longer spoken. I admit, Lope, that I do not fully understand this but I know that when I speak Spanish I do feel closer to my people and I do not think the gringo feels the same way when he speaks English.

"'And that is why later Señor Lopez invited me to studied Nahuatl so that I might better understand the roots of our culture but I never did because my life became very busy working two jobs, my day job as a carpenter and my evening job as a salad sandwich maker. So I had no time to attend Señor Lopez's lessons which he gave in his store in the evening. I had very little time for myself. All I did was work and sleep but I visited him when I could and read very many of his books. I often thought he must have read all of the books in his store for he was a very wise man and I was very fortunate to have such a wise man as my mentor.'

"'What do you mean, Papa? Will I not meet this man because now I think I would like to study the mother tongue of our people, Nahuatl?'

"'No, *mijo*, you will not because he died two years before I came to get you. But the store remains though Nahuatl is no longer taught there. But I shall try to be to you the mentor he was to me and if you desire to learn *la lengua Mexicana* there is man who now teaches it the Latino Cultural Center.

"'Yes, Papa, I would like that.'

"'So you see, Lope, the idea of the cockroach people has been around since even before you were born and today it is well known among the Mexican people living in the U.S. and among the intelligentsia in Mexico. It is a different way of understanding *El Movimiento* which is no longer simply a revolt but an invasion. What is happening is understood and supported by the most important politicos such as Vicente Fox and all the Latino politicians north and south of the border like the California Assembly Speaker Fabian Núñez, *un teniente en El Movimiento* who discusses with a wink and a nod the Latino invasion with *Presidente* Vicente Fox. I can just hear what he tells the *Generalísimo, that everything is going as planned and not to worry about the fuming gringos because we are millions strong.* That's why *teniente* Núñez receives the red-carpet treatment when he visits his homeland because he represents the Mexican people not the American gringo.

"'Listen to this, *mijo*. I was told by an amigo who knows many things about *El Movimiento* that *Presidente* Fox has a map of the United States in what he calls the War Room. And this map shows all the counties and cities in all the states of the U.S. The counties and cities in white are still mostly gringo, and the ones in blue are mostly black, of which there are only a few dozen, and now I do not think New Orleans will remain blue because I think it will be reoccupied not by black Americans but illegal Mexican workers who will get the construction jobs when the city is rebuilt because American businessmen love Latino workers who work very hard for very little and do not require benefits which they get anyway from all kinds of social programs for the poor paid for by gringo taxpayers.

"'You see, Lope, even if Latino workers are in the country illegally they can still buy homes often at discounted interest rates with the help of gringo politicos, such as the Governor of Illinois Rod Blagojevich, and government organizations such as the Fed's HUD and state Housing Development Authorities, and homegrown leftist organizations like ACORN, all of which use gringo tax dollars to enable illegal immigrants to plant permanent roots in America. And of course greedy gringo banks like Wells Fargo, Citibank, and Hemlock Federal Bank, a bank named after the plant that caused the death of the philosopher Plato, the plant we call *la cicuta*, fall over themselves to give illegal immigrants loans for their new homes. It is not difficult to see how such banks are a kind of poison to gringo communities, though in New Orleans the black communities shall be the ones to disappear. And, Lope, do you know why the banks are a kind of poison?

"'I think so, Papa. It is because what banks love most is money. That is no secret.'

"'Yes, it is no secret. Still an unwise person would not have known this, Lope. That is why Jesus compared tax collectors to sinners and prostitutes, because they loved money above all else, and that is why if Jesus were alive today he would scorn bankers as he scorned tax collectors in his own time. But America has become a nation of tax collectors, that is a nation of businessmen who love money more than they love their own people, who in truth they do not love at all. Have you not heard of ENRON, Lope?'

"'No, Papa, I have not.'

"'Well it was and remains the model for American business. The government did not care that it broke the law because it gave politicians *mucho dinero*. It was only when it lost money and became an embarrassment that the government stepped in. Of course the *puercos* who ran the company left with their pockets full. Americans complain about the drug cartels but they are no worse than American businesses. In fact they are not so bad as the American drug companies because the cartels would not seek to profit from the suffering and death of the elderly. And everyone knows the American government cares nothing about the elderly or the poor until they become an embarrassment like those floating bodies in New Orleans.

"'But after New Orleans is rebuilt it will be a new Hispanic city and it will be better than before because Mexicans will not allow such a thing to happen, not if we have the power to save lives, which the American government had at the time. Nor do we take from the black people anything that would not have been taken sooner or later by the Vietnamese who already occupy New Orleans East. So our victory in New Orleans will be a great victory for Mexico and the Mexican people because another American city will have become a brown one.

"'A brown one, Papa?'

"'Yes, Lope. You see, the counties and cities which are brown on *Presidente* Fox's map are Latino and now cover much of the U.S. and each year they increase as our people spread throughout the U.S. My friend says that every time the Latinos conquer a new county or city Vicente Fox and his politico friends get together to celebrate. Smoking their Cuban cigars and sipping Jose Cuervo Reserva tequila they salute *El Movimiento*. Then the *Presidente* is asked to predict the next county or city to become Latino. At this moment my friend says the crowd becomes quiet with anticipation. Then the *Presidente* smiles broadly and points to the map to a place such as Costa Mesa, San Juan Capistrano, or San Bernardino, which now has a Latina mayor. And when he calls out its name all present give out a big cheer because, so my friend says, the *Presidente* has never been wrong.'

"'But, Papa, how could he never be wrong?'

"'For this reason, Lope, one cannot make a river flow back to its home in the mountains once it has found its new home in the valley.'

"'And do the gringos know of this map?'

"'No, as I have said many times, the gringos don't have the sense of donkeys which is perhaps an unfair thing to say about donkeys who are really a very fine animal but as you know it is only a way of speaking. Of course *Presidente* Fox and his friends do not speak of these things publicly only in private.'

"'*El Movimiento*,' repeated Lope. I could see that he like myself was taken by the word so he asked to know more about it. And Arsenio said it pleased him very much that his son took an interest in the serious matters of which he spoke. So he continued.

"'Do you remember when I spoke of Villaraigosa being *un soldado en El Movimiento*, though now he is general, a *jefe*?' Yes, Lope remembered.

"'It is the campaign of the cockroach people,' continued Arsenio, 'to recapture Aztlán,' but Lope said he had never heard of Aztlán before and was still unsure of its meaning and Arsenio said that is why he came for him so that he would know such things and become a part of the greatest event for Mexicans since *La Independence*. Then he went on to explain his meaning.

"'You know of the revolt of 1810?' he asked.

"'Yes of course,' said Lope, 'the Mexicans revolted against the *gachupines*.'

"'Exactly,' said Arsenio. 'Well *El Movimiento* is another great battle for independence. Just as our forefathers took back their land from the Spanish we will take back our land from the American gringos.'

"'And Vicente Fox knows of this?' asked Lope, still surprised that such a thing was possible.

"'Of course he does. All the Mexican politicians know this and when they talk privately they laugh about the fat gringos and their greedy American *politicastros* who serve themselves, not their people.'

"'*El Movimiento*,' repeated Lope, now very much fascinated. 'But how is it possible, Papa? The Americans have the most powerful army in the world.'

"'But, Lope, their armies are helpless against civilian *soldados* who are presently invading the U.S. That is what our politicians understand. Mexican soldiers could never win against the American war machine but the army of the people *will* win, and it will even be helped by American Republicans who love money more than they love people and by the American Democrats led by American Jews to create a multicultural America, an American Babel, a land of a thousand tongues, in which English will become just another language of many, a language of convenience, and the gringos will become one minority among many.

"'Like us, the Jews, who contributed heavily to Villaraigosa's victory in L.A., do not respect gringos but not for the same reason. For us they are thieves who stole part of our homeland but the Jews despise the gringos as the swindler despises the sucker, the *bobo* he cheats. They have sold the gringo on the multicultural dream to benefit themselves. But it is a fool's errand for the gringos who have forgotten that to be divided is to be conquered. And one day they will awake from their dream to find themselves in a multicultural nightmare they will not be able to awake from. They are a foolish people who are impossible to respect. But the *nortemejicanos* are not foolish and the gringo's nightmare will be a dream come true for all *mejicanos*, the return of Aztlán to its rightful owners.

"'Then the gringo will come to us and complain like Job complained to God that he was treated unfairly. He will say that the Mexicans had no right to steal America from the Americans. But then we will explain to the gringo that he is a hypocrite because he supported the Jews' right to Palestine because it was once their homeland, and because two thousand years have passed since that time, the Americans should support even more our claim to *Aztlán*, which was taken from the Mexican people just one hundred and fifty years ago.

"'But the gringo will not listen because the Jews' repossession of Palestine did not harm the gringo, only the Palestinians. But our repossession of *Aztlán* does affect the gringo squatters in California, Utah, Nevada, Arizona, New Mexico, Colorado, and Texas, which are the pieces of the ancient *Aztlán* puzzle. They will claim that we have no right to our homeland which they stole from us but how can they say that when they supported the Jews right to their homeland? They cannot.

"'And like the Jews we have sought to divide America and doing so have united ourselves. And our success is seen and heard everywhere. But the truth is that though more than a hundred tongues are now spoken in American schools America is not multilingual but truly only bilingual. Spanish is now taught in every high school in America along side English— not Hebrew, not Arabic, not Chinese, not German, and of course not French which is now a dead language in America because Americans believe the French are their enemy. That's why if you were to meet their *Presidente* Señor Bush he would greet you saying *buenos días,* not *bonjour,* not only because he hates the French but because Spanish is America's *nueva lengua materna.*

"'He is a very stupid gringo. He hates the French who invade only with wine and cheese and loves his conquerors and brags that he can speak their language but had he read a book on history he'd know that when you speak the language of the invader you've been conquered. Just as the Ancient peoples conquered by the Romans learned to speak Latin so the Americans learned to speak Spanish. But then maybe Señor Bush is not so stupid after all but knows which way the *dinero* wind is blowing, from the south.

"'You know the old saying, Lope, *if you cannot beat them join them,* so Señor Bush says the U.S. government should create a *guest worker program* that will allow millions of illegal immigrants to work and live in the U.S. legally. That way like the smart political fox he is he keeps everybody happy: the foolish gringos who believe the immigrants will one day go home because they are called *guests,* the Mexicans who are in the country illegally but will one day become U.S. citizens, the gringo businessmen who love money more than they love their people, and the gringo politicians who love Latino votes as much as the businessmen love money.

"'Señor Bush even appointed a Mexican as the U.S. Attorney General, Mr. Alberto R. Gonzales, so the top cop in America is one of our own. It is true Señor Bush looks and sounds like a buffoon but what he desires most in life are money and power and now he has very much of both. I don't think he is so stupid nor is his family. When he was a big oil man in Midland, Texas, his company preferred hiring Mexican workers to work in the oil fields because they were cheap and I believe many were illegal. But of course Señor Bush knows nothing about that just as he knew nothing about the leaking of classified information that blew the cover of CIA agent Valerie Plame. And when he looked about the town of Midland, it was for him like looking into a crystal ball that showed that the future of America was not gringo, but Latino.

"'And so seeing the future he knew that speaking the language of the future would be to his financial and political advantage. So before he became governor of Texas he drove all over Texas promoting his baseball team the Texas Rangers. But of course a Texas big shot does not want to be seen driving his own car so Señor Bush hired a Latino chauffeur but this man was not just Bush's chauffeur. He was also his Spanish teacher. And that is why Bush was able to speak Spanish to all the Latinos living in America when he was campaigning to become *Presidente* Bush.

"'And when the former governor of California wanted to deny illegal immigrants public services paid for by gringo taxpayers Señor Bush told him very publicly in front of many other governors and all the media that he was wrong. And do you know why he said this, Lope? Because he knew he would one day need the Latino vote to become *el presidente*. And when he was finally campaigning to become *el presidente de Estados Unidos de América* he proclaimed to his rival Senator Pat Buchanan the last American politico who might have saved America for Americans, *"No cheap shots at Mexico."*

"'But what most astonished me, Lope, was seeing Señor Bush in one of his campaign videos. In that video he was hugging a Mexican woman and holding a Mexican baby just as any gringo politician would have done. So that was not what surprised me. What surprise me was seeing Señor Bush waving a Mexican flag and I do not think any other American politician would have done that unless he was Latino, of course. It was then I knew whose side Señor Bush was on and which side would win. That is why, Lope, I believe the birth of the American Hispanic Nation is occurring during the reign of *Presidente* Bush. It is a painful birth but only for the gringos.'

"Arsenio sat back for a moment smiling and thinking about what he had said. Perhaps in his mind he was seeing Señor Bush waving the Mexican flag. Lope watched him and then said 'It is truly amazing that the American president would be on the side of those who invade his country.'

"'It is not just him, Lope but his entire family. They love foreigners because they make them even richer than they already are. His father loves the Saudis because he is in the oil business and the Saudis have the most oil. And like his father and brother, Jeb Bush must have seen that in the near future American business and politics would become Latino business and politics because he married a Mexican-born Latina and moved to Miami which is a Latino city, Cuban but Latino nonetheless. And look at him now. He's governor of Florida which is quickly becoming a Latino state and is already a state where Señor Jeb Bush and the American *presidente* are very popular. Of course both these men preach the gospel of open immigration laws. You see, Lope, the more Latinos the more votes for *la familia de Bush*. So it will not surprise me if Jeb Bush becomes the next *presidente* of the United States or that the first Latino *presidente* of the United States is also a Bush, Señor George P. Bush, the governor's son. In fact, Lope, the only thing that surprises me is that the little flag that *Presidente* Bush wears on his lapel is not the Mexican flag.'

"'That is all very amazing to me, Papa. It almost seems that they sold out their countrymen.'

"'So it seems, Lope, and that is why *Presidente* Bush is not our friend but our *títere*, our puppet. He uses us for his financial and political gain and we use him for the advancement of our people and the repossession of *Aztlán*. Yes, Lope, you are right. The difference between us and Señor Bush is that we serve our people and he serves himself, his family, and his cronies. He is an American Judas. No, Lope, that is not fair to Judas, who betrayed Jesus in order serve him. Bush betrayed America in order to serve himself, his family, and his cronies.

"'And if his nephew does not become the first Latino American president it will not matter because the Latino people in America are now in control of their own destiny and that of America. I will give you an example, the governor of New Mexico Señor Bill Richardson. His name is that of an anglo but his mother was Mexican and his father was born in Nicaragua. He is one of us. In New Mexico he has welcomed the illegal immigrants from Mexico, given to them the right to have a driver's license and to their children the right to go to school even if they too are illegal. And now he is considering running for president of the United States. *Se hará*, Lope. *It will be done* in your lifetime the first Latino president. Then our eagle shall fly away with the gringo serpent in its claw and release it in the desert where it will live the best it can or die.'

"'I cannot believe all the things you have told me, Papa, though I do.'

"'They are true, Lope. I shall now tell you of an experience I had that was to me almost like a vision. Shortly before I came to you I went to an art gallery in L.A. that shows the work of new Latino painters and there I saw a painting called *The Beginning of the End*. It showed a beautiful Latina woman who was in the sky looking down upon L.A. which had become a city of barrios, the walls of the buildings covered with beautiful murals and the streets filled with hundreds, thousands, of colorful Latino figures. It was a very beautiful and very spiritual painting like Mexico itself but at first I did not know what the title meant. Then I realized it was the beginning of the end of the gringo's rule in L.A. I stood before that painting for a very long time. It was to me as the figure of the Virgin of Guadalupe is to the old women of the church. It was a sacred thing this painting. In it I could see clearly the end of the gringo and a new beginning for our own people. The painting made me feel very wonderful.'

"Arsenio then looked to the ground, smiling and shaking his head as if in disbelief. Then he looked a Lope and said 'It is a wonder, Lope, that the gringo people are so ignorant with all their money and schools. Still shaking his head and smiling he said 'They prance like stallions but we see they are all donkeys, not even donkeys.' Then his smile went away and he said 'They are pitiful but we will show them no pity because they are thieves. They call us thieves but they stole the land of the Indians and they stole our land. They are the thieves, and they show pity to no one. They treat our workers as slaves as they do the workers of the world. They gobble up all the riches of the world. They are *comelones*, gluttons.'

"And you know it is true, Señor Thomas. You gringos have so much, but are never satisfied."

"Imelda, just finish your story about Arsenio. It's bad enough listening to his criticism of us gringos."

"Yes, of course, Señor Thomas. So Arsenio continued, 'Lope, we are not alone in our struggle. We are united with our Spanish speaking allies from Cuba, Puerto Rico, Guatemala, El Salvador, Honduras, Nicaragua, and other Latinos south of the border. And each day they arrive by the thousands into the U.S. and join the millions-strong army of the cockroach people. Now even the Brazilians enter America by the thousands. It's true they are not true Hispanics because they speak Portuguese but they are more Latino than gringo.'

"'But the Latino army is an army without guns,' said Lope."

"'Lope, I will tell you a secret. Though it may seem that we are just innocent, unarmed civilians, truly we have many armies of our own in America that have guns, hundreds of Latino gangs, tens of thousands of *vatos locos*, with more arriving each day. Our insurgency will drive the gringo from our barrios and the millions of Latino voters will drive out of office all the gringo politicians and judges and police chiefs and all the other gringo *burcóratas*. We have many weapons, Lope, but like the gringo's president says, out greatest weapon is democracy. *Viva La Democracia!* In other words we are going to vote ourselves into power. We shall overcome, Lope, with bullets *and* ballots. And the gringos will even give us ballots written in Spanish to vote them out of office.'

"'The gringos are a very strange people, Papa. They are like *los leminos* that run to the sea and drown.'

"'That is true, Lope. The gringo seems to seek his destruction as the lemmings do, always running away from what he was to something new whereas our people seek to preserve what we were and are. That is why we seek to reclaim *Aztlán*. We Mexicans do not wish to run away from who we are for to do so would mean to commit suicide as a people. The *lemming people*—that is a very good name for the gringo, Lope.'

"And when Arsenio said this he smiled a sad thoughtful smile. I think he was please with the cleverness of his son. I did not know what the sadness was for. I thought maybe it was for you gringos but that is impossible. How can one feel sadness for that which one hates?'

"Tell me, Imelda, do you hate us as much as your husband does?"

"Sometimes I think I do, Señor Thomas, but I do not hate you or your family. What we do is necessary."

"What do you mean *What we do is necessary*? I don't understand."

"I will tell you but first let me finish my story about what Arsenio told his son."

"Oookay," I said resignedly. "What more did Arsenio have to say about us lemming gringos?"

"Next he spoke of a *compañero* who also thinks you gringos are a very strange people."

"'You know, Lope, when I came on this journey to get you, I stayed with an *amigo* Leonardo Rodriguez in Santa Ana, a town in Orange County, which has become famous because of the TV show *O.C.* Not long ago Santa Ana was a gringo town but no longer. Even its mayor Miguel Pulido is one of us, an immigrant from Mexico City. Today seventy-seven percent of its people speak Spanish and over half were not born in the U.S. Leonardo was *un compañero* on my first journey north and now has a very big house that once belonged to a gringo family. He said living in Santa Ana was just like living in Mexico except he made more money. And he is right. All the signs in the city are in Spanish and the businesses are named after towns in Mexico. It's just like Mexico. Oh Lope, the gringo is so blind. We tell him we are proud to be Mexican-American but the truth is that we are proud to be Mexicans living in America and one day there will be no difference between the big Mexico to the south and the little Mexico in the north and in a few years it will not be so little.

"'That evening Leonardo and I sat in his beautiful backyard and drank Coronas while his wife and daughters prepared an exquisite meal in my honor. We talked of the things I am now speaking of to you and he said to me "The gringos are a very strange people; they just give away their towns. Arsenio, I could take you to another town just a few miles away and you would think you were in Vietnam. The city is Westminster named I think after a town in London but now, it's so funny, they call it Little Saigon and for good reason. It's just as much Saigon as Santa Ana is Apatzingan or Zamora or Patzcuaro. And you know that Vietnamese boat people continue to arrive in America though the Vietnam War has been over for thirty-five years. I tell you, Arsenio, *los extranjeros* here are the gringos."

"'I said I knew of the boat people's arrival to LAX and that I agreed with him, saying that the gringos are indeed very strange but also *mentecato*. And I explained to Leonardo that in L.A. there are signs that say *Los Angeles, Mexico,* and at one train station a monument says *This land was Mexican once, was Indian always and is, and will be again.* Can you believe that gringo money paid for such a thing! Of course some gringos are offended but that will change nothing. L.A. is a Latino city that was once controlled by the gringos but no longer.

"'Leonardo laughed and said "It is the same in Westminster where the Vietnamese want to change the American street signs to Vietnamese, such as Moran Street, which was named after the founder of Westminster, an Irishman I think. They want to change it to Yen Do Street. One day I expect that they will want to change John Wayne Airport to Ngo Dinh Diem Airport.

Ha ha ha . . . ." Leonardo laughed again because the name was a tongue twister for him.

"'"My English is not so good but in Santa Ana I am able to speak my own language. And Arsenio, what you say about signs is true in Westminster as well. It was a gringo college professor who proposed the changing of the name. I tell you the gringos have no pride, no *patriotismo*."

"'"That is because they have no sense of *la familia*, no sense of *la comunidad*," I said to Leonardo. And really, Lope, the language of the street signs does not matter because even if the street signs are not changed Westminster will remain a Vietnamese city and the English names of streets . . . well, they will become ghosts of what once was but is no more. And the reason for this is that at heart gringos are lone wolves. They have always been a people on the move who have little attachment to any place. They truly are the migrant people.'

"'But, Papa, we too are migrants, yes?'

"'That is a very good point, Lope. But it only appears that way. The Mexican people who migrate to the U.S. do not leave Mexico because they carry Mexico within their hearts. Besides what appears to be a leaving is in fact our people returning to their ancient homeland *Aztlán*. And I tell you this, Lope, with our blood and our souls we will reclaimed our homeland and once we have done so it shall be us, not the Vietnamese, who will change the name of John Wayne Airport. Perhaps to Emiliano Zapata Airport, a true patriot and hero, not a fake one like John Wayne who fought for his country only in the movies.'

"'I did not know that, Papa. I always thought John Wayne was a true American hero.'

"'That is what the gringos like to believe but they live in a fantasy world. Even today they have a paper soldier for president. Every day I thank God that I am not a gringo.

"'You know, Lope, Leonardo has seven daughters and each one is beautiful and a wonderful cook. I know he loves them very much but the poor man wanted a son. "We kept trying," he told me, "but finally we decided that it was God's will that we have only daughters." I personally think that his wife just did not have it in her to produce a son and I tell you, Lope, I would not trade you for ten daughters. But I did not say that to Leonardo. I told him that his bad luck was God's will because it was good for *El Movimiento*. Just do the math, Lope. Seven times seven is forty-nine, times seven is three hundred and forty-three, times seven is hundreds more, time seven is thousands. And do you know, Lope, *las latinas* in Santa Ana between the ages 15 and 19 also have *mucho niños*, twice the national average. And then consider also that a million Latinos enter the country illegally each year.

"'You see the math is not on the side of the gringo who will soon be a minority in his own country, a tiny marshmallow in a big cup of hot chocolate. And that tiny marshmallow grows smaller each day and not just for the American gringos but for the European gringos as well. Not long ago I read in the *Los Angeles Times* that in 1950 the European gringos made up twenty-two percent of the world's population. Today less than eleven percent and forty-five years from now the European gringos will represent only seven percent of the world's population. I tell you, Lope, the gringos of the world are quickly going the way of the dinosaur.'

"'But how is that possible, Papa? The gringo peoples have ruled the world forever.'

"'In truth, Lope, the gringos have not ruled the world for so very long and for a very short time in the Americas and their decline means only that the world is returning to the way it always has been. Like albinos the gringo is a freak of nature, an abnormality.'

"'And is that why the gringos will soon disappear from the earth like the dinosaurs?'

"'The problem, Lope, is that the gringo is impotent, at most one or two children often none. The gringos fuck a lot but produce few children so it must be God's will. He does not bless a sick people. So we will win the war against the gringo with bullets, ballots, *and* babies.'

"'Still, Papa, it's strange that the gringos would do nothing, that they would allow themselves to be overrun by the cockroach people as you call us.'

"'It seems so, Lope, but it is the same reason God gives them only *pocos niñōs*. I will explain. The gringos are too decadent, too *depravado* to do anything. Most are too busy watching their big televisions and eating pizza and burgers and drinking Budweiser *cerveza* to pay us much notice. You know, the gringo is always speaking of the corruption in Mexico but the corruption in Mexico is only among the politicians and *capitalistas grasa*, just as in the U.S., but the Mexican people are not corrupt. In America the disease of corruption is a plague among the gringos. They even have a word for the sickness, *affluenza*.'

"'Like influenza,' said Lope.

"'Exactly except that it sickens the soul rather than the body. It is like a fever that causes the sick one never to be satisfied never to be still. These people are like *hormigas*, always busy being busy but they are worse because the *hormigas* rest in the winter and work for the colony as the Mexican people do. In fact I do not think any of nature's creatures are like the gringo because nature's creatures are not depraved. Perhaps a disease such as cancer which is never satisfied until it causes death. *Affluenza* is a disease of unsatisfied desire. *El consumo* has become a way of life for the gringo because I think gringos are no longer a people of the land and village. They sold out the old ways and in doing so sold their souls. They are hollow, a forest of dead trees, their insides eaten out by the termites of desire. They try to fill the emptiness with impedimenta but the hollowness is never filled because it can never be filled with such things. But this the gringo does not understand. So he'll continue searching for things to fill the emptiness and continue to fail because he no longer knows what is of value, that which gave his life meaning before emptiness came.

"'I'm not sure I understand, Papa.'

"'I will give you an example, my son. You have heard of Wal-Mart yes?'

"'Of course,' said Lope, 'everyone has heard of Wal-Mart. They are the monster stores that are as big as villages and filled with everything sold under the sun.'

"'Yes they are famous throughout the world. Well the gringos love Wal-Mart even though as you said they are monster stores as big as a village but they also contain the merchandise of a hundred small towns so that when one is built all the small towns and their mom-and-pop stores miles and miles around wither and die. And if a Wal-Mart is built in a big city hundreds of little businesses die. That is how Wal-Mart is a monster, a devilfish, its tentacles reaching far out beyond itself destroying towns and businesses and with them the old ways of living and doing business. Of course the old culture dies and all that is left is an ugly box the size of a village. But gringos do not care as long as they can buy cheap. They do not seem to know that what they buy is not so cheap but has cost them dearly. In order to buy cheaper toothpaste or cheaper CDs they have sold the souls of their communities.

"'Have you never heard the story of Faust, Lope?'

"'No' said Lope.

"'Well Faust was a man who sold his soul to the devil.'

"'Why would a man ever do such a thing?' ask Lope very much astounded by the idea.

"'Because Faust wanted everything and was willing to trade his soul for all the things he desired. But of course once he gave up his soul he discovered that everything would not fill the hollowness created by the absence of his soul.'

"'Why is that?' asked Lope.

"'Because your soul is your true self and dwells deep within you like a spring and nourishes all that you do so that you become something truly, something more than just having money, having sex, having a fancy car, having this and that, but being something truly. But you must find your soul because it flows quietly and you must drink from it all your life.

"'And Faust did not do this?' asked Lope.

"'No, he did not. He lost his soul and went to hell. But you see, Lope, the moral of the story is that hell is not a place. Hell is losing yourself. And, Lope, can you tell me why losing yourself would be hell?'

"'I think because then you are nothing' said Lope gravely.

"'I was right to return to Mexico for my son because he is wise and will become wiser' said Arsenio. And I could see, Señor Thomas, that Arsenio loved his son very much. Then he went on about the gringo.

"'You see, Lope, the gringo is not wise. He is like a man who thinks he's wise, who is puffed up like a puffer fish with pride but he is truly empty within because he has traded his soul for things, the things that fill his monster stores. There are many monsters in the U.S. Wal-Mart is only one. So the gringo's hollowness will continue to grow but we Mexicans are not lost.

"'We are like the mountain lion and the coyote, like the hawk and the woodpecker, the butterfly and the scorpion, the lizard and the snake, the cactus and the sunflower, like all of nature's creatures who know who they are. We know where we must go, what we must do, and what we must not do. And most of all we must be careful not to catch the gringo sickness. Many years ago another great general of *El Movimiento* Rodolfo Gonzales warned the Mexican people about the sickness of the gringos, a sickness the entire world fears today. And this is very important, Lope, so listen carefully,' and Lope leaned a little closer to his father to show that he was very interested.

"'Gonzales said that the gringo society is a sick society, that the gringos have achieved great technological progress but at the expense of their souls, like the body builders who use steroids that make their muscles very big but cause their *cajones* to wither like dried grapes and become impotent.

"'One day, Lope, I will take you where you can see clearly what has happened to the gringo—Las Vegas—a mecca for the spiritually dead, a city of whores and pimps, where the glutton gringos swill booze, take drugs, and have sex and lose their money and lives. A city that brags *"What happens in Vegas stays in Vegas."* You see, Lope, cities are a bigger version of people. So when you go to Las Vegas it is like looking at the gringo under a microscope. You can see what he really is, or perhaps I should say what he has become.'

"'Papa, I'm not sure what you mean. I think I would like to go to Las Vegas but you say it is a city of the dead.'

"'The dead are without souls and by that I mean the gringos have lost their way because they have lost the old ways, the ways rooted in the land, village, and people. As you know *Las Vegas* means fertile fields but no longer. In that place what now grows is corruption. In order not to face their emptiness the hollow gringos must keep buying things and keep being entertained; otherwise their emptiness will swallow them like the whale swallowed Jonah and in the darkness they will be terrified and lose their minds. So they must always be distracted by this or that in order to stay ahead of the dark whale that seeks to swallow them into darkness. Thus they have become addicted to the very thing that destroys them. They complain that the immigrants will destroy them and we will but they are already mostly dead from their own sickness.

"'That is why Gonzales warned that the greatest danger of the gringo people is not their police, not their army, not their government—because those things cannot destroy the Chicano people. It is their spiritual sickness that can destroy the people of *Aztlán*. That is why we must stay with our own people and protect our culture from the gringo sickness. You say you would like to go to Las Vegas and we will. But you must remember that the beautiful city that sparkles with a million lights on the desert is a mirage, a fata morgana, that promises happiness but gives only despair.'

"'So America is like the mirage of a lake seen by a man dying of thirst?'

"'Yes, it can be that, a lake of salt.'

"'But America is real not an illusion.'

"'Of course but remember that the harm of the mirage is that it leads the thirsty man in the wrong direction. It is a beautiful thing to look upon but it doesn't give what a man truly thirsts for.'

"'What is that, Papa?'

"'The old ways rooted in the land, the village, and the people. It is the culture passed on from generation to generation, a culture rooted in the earth and the ways of the earth, not the culture of manufactured dreams designed and created by those who make money from selling them and make slaves of those who buy them.'

"'This thing is perhaps too difficult for me to understand, Papa.'

"'No it's not. Let me approach it from another direction. Does the carnival still come to Asolaca?'

"'Of course. Did you not go when you lived in Asolaca?'

"'Yes many times but tell me, Lope, what was the most fun for you?'

"'I liked the animals especially the lion and elephant and the camel which you could ride. And the mechanical rides of course such as the Ferris wheel and octopus.'

"'Yes I remember all that. And the haunted house, does it still exist?'

"'Yes but it's less scary when you are older.'

"'And are there still the freak shows with the likes of the fat bearded lady and the tattooed man?'

"'No, Papa. All the women are fat today though they don't have beards, perhaps a small mustache.' Saying this Lope smiled at his little joke and I was very happy to see he had a sense of humor. Then he continued. 'I think the gangsters who wear tattoos today are more scary than the tattooed man you saw at the old carnival. But there was one tent that contained many dead babies in jars.'

"'I remember that yes. And of course there are still games of skill that you can play to win a stuffed animal or a fish that would be dead the next day.'

"'You are very funny, Papa. I like that. Yes the games still exist and the fish always die.'

"'And so the people leave their village, their homes, and their work to go to the carnival. Why do they do that, Lope?'

"'You know, Papa, to have fun of course. To escape from real life for an evening because life is not so easy for the people in the village.'

"'And so the carnival is not real life, Lope?'

"'In a way no. For the people who work for the carnival maybe but for the others it's just make-believe.'

"'Like daydreams, a pleasant place to visit.

"'Yes, Papa.'

"'And tell me, Lope. Did you ever think about running away with the carnival?'

"'Yes after returning home and lying in bed and thinking about the same old life in Asolaca.'

"'I understand. Life in the village is not so exciting or as much fun as the carnival and as you say, it is not so easy. So it is to be expected that you would sometimes wish to go off with the carnival and become what the gringos call carnies, people of the carnival. Then you could play the games and go on the rides and visit the freak shows all you want.'

"'Yes, Papa, that is what I have thought many times.'

"'But those who join the carnival leave the village and the old ways and become nomads living in a fantasy world of merrymaking not for a day or a week but for a lifetime. They are no longer rooted in the real world because they are always on the move. They are a people who are disconnected. They have become strangers in the world.'

"'Is that such a bad thing, Papa?'

"'Not for a few I suppose who are always restless. But I will tell you this because I gave it some thought when I visited the big fairs and circuses in America. These carnies do not seem so happy to me. They have hard looks, the looks people have when they have lived too long alone in the world cut off from family, friends, and neighborhood—the roots that nourish a life, the things people go back to after visiting the carnival.

"'My grandfather, who died some years before you were born, told me once that a man must always have a garden. At first I thought the idea was silly because tending a garden is a woman's job but I never said that because I respected my *abuelito* but I came to understand his meaning once I came to the U.S. I felt lost for a while like a piece of litter blown in the wind but soon I found the barrio and my roots began to grow once more.'

"'Is land for gardens to be found in the city, Papa?'

"'Not so much, *mijo*, but what my grandfather meant was that one's people, *la raza*, is the garden that one must tend and like a garden it will support and nourish you. But do not worry, Lope, because many Latino gardens await us in America and they grow larger each day. We have left your old village but will soon be in the barrio of L.A.'

"'And the gringos do they not also have their garden?'

"'No, *mijo*, they do not because they have become carnies and carnivalites. This is strange because the gringos are very clever but they are not wise. If they were they would not allow us to take back the land that belongs to us.'

"'And why is it, Papa, that they do not fight to keep what is now their homeland?'

"'I think it's because of what I have been telling you. When you go to the carnival do you take your worries with you?'

"'No. You go to the carnival to forget your worries.'

"'Yes, *mijo*, that is correct. But now tell me why it is important that a carnival pack up and leave.'

"'I know, Papa, so that the people will return to their village like the gardener who must return to his garden so that it will not die.'

"'Oh *mijo*, I see that you are a very fast learner like your father which is essential in life because knowledge is your weapon and your shield. And somehow this is what the gringo has forgotten and it is that most of all that makes him helpless against us.'

"'But how could the gringos forget something so important?'

"'You see, Lope, some time ago the gringos went to the carnival and stayed or perhaps the carnival came to America and never left. That is what you see clearly in a city like Las Vegas, a city that has become a carnival. The gringos themselves call it *sin city* but it is the fastest growing and most visited city in America. Las Vegas is what America has become, a culture without a soul. And if you were God and could listen to Las Vegas as we listen to the conch… but first tell me what it is you hear when you listen to the *caracol de mar*, Lope?'

"'You hear the sea, Papa. Everyone knows that.'

"'Exactly it's a great thing really. But if you were God and held Las Vegas to your ear do you know what you would hear?'

"'No, Papa. What?'

"'You would hear a hollow sound, an emptiness.'

"'But do not the gringos hear it, Papa?'

"'No they do not because their culture is full of noise.'

"Aah, I think I understand your meaning, Papa.'

"'But there is more, Lope. Now the carnival has entered into their homes through the television, the DVD, the computer, the stereo. The carnival in America has become a devilfish like Wal-Mart. Even in their homes the gringos have forgotten about the garden of the family and friends and community, all that Mexicans value. That is why America is the land of opportunity but also an insidious place for Mexicans. For the gringo it is too late. For them it is the land of the living dead. That is why I have no sympathy for the gringo.

"'They gave up the garden and for what, my son? A life without substance, without permanence. They dream their empty dreams but when they awake they will discover they have nothing, only a shell made of those things which are purchased.

"'And the reason I tell you this is so that you will not be drawn into the carnival of the gringos and forget who you really are because once you forget who you are you are nothing.'

"'But…but Papa, if you mean forget that I am a Mexican you do not have to worry. I would never forget such a thing.'

"'That is true, Lope, but only as long as you live among your own people. Do you remember Señor Lopez I told you about, the wise man who helped me to learn English?'

"'Yes, how could I forget such a man?'

"'It was from him that I first heard of how the gringos have become a hollow people but he explained these things to me in a very funny way. He called the gringos the *sopaipilla* people and said that gringos behave the way they do because they are always trying to fill the emptiness within them. And then he explained that when a people have lost their souls they are reduced to their stomachs because they have nothing else to live for. That is why the gringos are *mucho obeso*, why their cars are so big, why their houses are never big enough, and why their garages are never big enough to contain all that they own. And of course as their stomachs grow larger and larger so do their appetites.'

"'Papa, I would think that they would eventually explode.'

"'You are very smart, Lope, to think that because they do in a way. They explode mentally by going crazy or physically by having a heart attack or financially by going broke. And in many other ways. Gringos love to preach about the family but their marriages do not last. They too explode. The parents separate from one another and the children separate from their parents.'

"'That's very sad is it not, Papa?'

"'Do not feel sad for the gringo, Lope. We love America but not the gringo because he is not our friend but our *adversario*. You have not forgotten what I said about Señor Darwin and his theory of evolution?'

"Of course not, Papa, because I can see by what you say that he is important.'

"'Very important. True he was a gringo but we Mexicans are wise to listen to those who speak wisely even if their people are our enemy. American gringos are very stupid because they think Señor Darwin is full of *frijoles* because he believed humans came from apes and not from God.'

"'And you, Papa, what do you believe?'

"'Well, *mijo*, I will speak honestly because I am your father and you are no longer a child. The stories about God the Father and Jesus and the Virgin are necessary deceptions for some especially women and children so that when life is very difficult they can believe that their father in the sky will help them. And if help is not possible they can look forward to living with all their family and friends in that happy place called heaven. And there are many other good things associated with the church such as having Sunday as a day of rest and the sacrament of marriage. And also one can learn much from the Bible about people.'

"'I have never read the Bible, Papa, but tell me, if you do not believe in God why do you speak of Him so often?'

"'It is sometimes a useful way of considering an important question. That is what your great-grandfather told me. *What would God think?* he would ask meaning how would a perfect being answer the question. Besides if you speak in the language of God then most people are more likely to listen to you. But if you speak in the language of the atheist then those very same people will ignore you and even hate you. But I think a father and son should speak honestly to one another. That is what I learned from your great-grandfather, who was a father to me. Of the Bible he said to me that it is worth reading but with many grains of salt as with any holy book. And it was he who taught me to read the Bible.'

"'Was he a holy man?'

"'Yes in his own way. But you know he never went to church. He liked the priest because it was said he had a mistress though he would not have liked the gringo priests who fondle the children in their care. Grandfather told me that I should read the Bible and while doing so put myself in the place of God as He looked down upon the ways of men. I asked him why I should do that and he said because what the Bible says that is most important is not about God but about men.'

"'And did you do this, Papa?'

"'Yes, but at first with *abuelito* then later on my own.'

"'And what did you learn by thinking like God?'

"'First I learned why God was so often angry because men were always doing evil. Then I learned that God really never existed except in the minds of men.'

"'Why, Papa?'

"'Because I understood that if God was so powerful he would have created a better world and better people for it so that people would not have to suffer so much by their own hand and so God would not have to punish so many people even those who never committed evil as he did when he flooded the world which killed children and animals as well as sinners. So I concluded that God was either very mean or stupid or did not exist. But a very mean or stupid God would not be God so I concluded that he must not exist.'

"'I see, Papa, but the thought of a world without God is very disturbing.'

"'Yes too much so for women and children but we are men. Tell me, Lope, do you know of *Nuestra Señora de Guadalupe*?'

"The Virgin of Guadalupe, of course. All Mexicans know of her.'

"'Very good but let me tell you something about her that you may not know."

"'Please do, Papa.'

"'First, it is a story like the many others told by the Catholic Church about visions and saints, and really they are all the same. Before the Virgin there was *Tonantzin*, the Aztec goddess of earth and corn who was also a virgin mother. Of course her worship was prohibited by the Church. However the Indians wanted very much to worship a holy mother for the same reason gods and goddesses are always worshipped by people who feel helpless in the face of things that threaten them. So one day…'

"'One moment, Papa. What is the reason the Virgin Mother is worshipped?'

"'Because she is the infinitely caring and powerful mother that children wish for as Jesus is the infinitely kind and powerful father.'

"'You mean to say that the worshippers are like children?'

"'Exactly. That is why such people call themselves the children of God. But let me finish my story.'

"'Yes, please.'

"'So the Catholic Church told the Indians that they could no longer worship their goddess because as you know the God of Christianity Himself said "I am a jealous God." Do you know how jealous, Lope?'

"'No, Papa, but I would like to know.'

"'So jealous of other gods that he warned that if parents disobey this commandment that he would punish their children.'

"'But that does not seem fair. I can hardly believe what you tell me.'

"'I know. It is unfair but that's what the Christian God said and as you know it is the very first of the Ten Commandments.'

"'Yes, I know that from what the priest said in church. *You shall have no gods before me, said the Lord.* But, Papa, you said that people desire an infinitely kind God to worship, a good divine parent not a mean one. I do not understand.'

"'You are correct, my son. The God of the Old Testament who is really the God of the Jews is very often a big bully. But think of this. How many Jews are there?'

"'Not so many because the Holocaust killed many millions of them?'

"'Yes, that is correct but would there have been many of them even if the Holocaust had not happened?'

"'No not so many.'

"'That is also correct and I will tell you why. Their God is too much a bully so you might say that Jesus was the new and improved version of the old bully that no one except the Jews felt comfortable doing business with. And of course added to the new and improved version was the Virgin. So the Christian religion offered exactly what poor and helpless people longed for—kindly, all-powerful parents.

"'But I will tell you a secret, Lope. It was not God who was jealous for what kind of God would become so upset by what ignorant, pitiful people think of Him? It was the Church. It is always the Church that is jealous, not God, because the Church like all human institutions seeks to preserve and expand its power. It is power that is the God of the Church. It is like the gringo *presidente* who seeks to control the world at least those places where money can be made and he carries the Bible with him everywhere he goes to show people that he is a good religious man.

"'And this brings me back to the story of the Virgin of Guadalupe. As I said the Catholic Church sought to control the Indians so it refused them their own gods and very cleverly substituted the Virgin Mary for their Tonantzin.'

"'But what of Juan Diego who saw the Virgin?'

"'He was a poor man and the poor see what their hearts desire. It is said that the Virgin told him that she wanted to be near his people to protect and love them but I believe *they wished* the Virgin to be near to love and protect them. In other words they gave birth to her. And did she protect them against the Spanish who stole their homeland, treated them like slaves, and took the harvest of their labor? No. She gave them hope and dreams and that is all. But I do not blame them. She was all they had and in their minds and hearts she was not so evil. She was evil only in the hands of priests and politicians and other exploiters of the people.'

"'And Darwin's ideas are not evil, Papa?'

"'Lope, strangely all ideas can be used for evil purposes even Señor Darwin's which have also been used to dominate and exploit.'

"'I think perhaps that it is better not to know anything, Papa.'

"'I understand your meaning, Lope. The truth is like a knife that cuts the tethers that bind us but in doing so wounds the flesh. That is why the gringos are afraid of the truth and like children hide beneath a blanket of lies told to them by their press and politicians and especially by their *presidente*, Señor Bush about the Glorious War against the terrorists of the world. And you can understand why the gringos want to believe that their children who are fighting, being mutilated, and dying in an unjust war are heroes. But the German people thought that their soldiers were heroes when they blitzkrieged into Poland and attacked Warsaw just as the gringos blitzkrieged into Iraq and attacked Baghdad. The German soldiers were not heroes because they served an evil man and did evil by attacking a country and destroying its cities though the country had done them no harm. And so the gringo soldiers are not heroes for the very same reason. Señor Bush is the gringos' führer and his Christian Coalition in truth is a Christian Reich.

"'The truth, Lope, is that the real heroes are those called by Señor Bush *insurgents*, the Iraqi Freedom Fighters who defend their people and faith from the anglo infidels who would take control of their country and its oil and eventually destroy their culture. But it is not only oil that is desired but also to protect Israel the beloved of America's Jews and Christian zealots. It is a joke when the American politicians say they care for the Iraqi people. They care no more for them than they do for us. It is money they care most about.

"'It is strange but the Iraqi freedom fighters remind me of the Warsaw Jews who revolted against the German occupiers during the famous Warsaw Uprising. Like those Jews the Iraqi insurgents are heroes not the gringo soldiers and their powerful military machine which have slaughtered Iraqis just as the Germans slaughtered the Polish Jews as a lawnmower cuts grass. And this is the truth Americans would rather not face.'

"'But, Papa, do not the Iraqi authorities support the gringo occupiers against the insurgents?'

"'Yes but the gringo imperialists do exactly what the German Nazis did. They set up a puppet government and use the police of the conquered people to enforce their control over them. When the Germans crushed the Jews in Warsaw they did so with the assistance of the Polish police and fire fighters.'

"'So, Papa, you are saying that if the gringos faced the truth about themselves they would see that they are just like the Nazi imperialists.'

"'That is correct, my son. Always remember that Americans are the descendants of imperialists who never left. The British finally left India; the French, Vietnam and Algeria; and the Spanish, Mexico; and so on, but the Europeans never left North America. They stayed as conquerors and became Americans but they do not want to see it that way. They prefer to see the destruction of the native peoples of North America as their glorious Manifest Destiny because there is no glory or honor in an evil war.'

"'Well I can see why the gringo prefers to hear lies rather than the truth.'

"Yes, and believe me they have been telling themselves lies ever since their European ancestors first set foot on North American soil. Not only did they believe that the destruction of nature and its native inhabitants was necessary they also believed it was a good thing that God required of them.'

"'How long can they hide from the truth, Papa?'

"'A very long time, forever for many. But the truth remains. Even if locked away behind lies truth's ghosts haunt the gringos and always will. So perhaps they are condemned to an existence of lies. Perhaps the truth is intended only for a courageous few because it always brings sadness even more so when one's own people are evil. As I have said, that is one reason for the make-believe in the Bible, to make people less sad. The inventors of the Bible were the ancient Jews. They were surrounded by Great civilizations such as Egypt, Babylonia, Assyria, Persia, and the empire of the Romans but they themselves were not a civilization only a tribe. They made no contribution to civilization which was done at the time mostly by the peoples of the great empires, especially the Greeks who were a most amazing people...'

"'But, Papa, the Bible is the most famous book in the world.'

"'That is true but let me finish, Lope.'

"'Yes, Papa.'

"'More than any other book the Bible has had a very big influence on the world but not a good influence because it caused the world to believe in a fictional fantasy rather than in what is truly real. It invented an imaginary being—God—and said that that imaginary being created the world which it didn't because God does not exist. And it gave credit to God that belongs to the mother of all things, nature...'

"'But, Papa, many people then believed in Gods."

"'That is a very good observation, Lope, but at the time educated people—mostly Greek philosophers—were ceasing to believe in those gods because they knew they were false. But then Christian Jews infected the thinking of the rulers of the Roman Empire who then banned the free thinking of the philosophers and scientists and replaced reality with a the fairy tales of the Bible...'

"'But why ban free thinking?'

"'Why do you think, Lope?'

"'Because when people think freely they ask too many questions.'

"'Yes, go on.'

"'And eventually the lie will be found out.'

"'Exactly, Lope. These free thinkers—the philosophers and scientists—were like detectives looking for the truth. And the power of the Church which had become very great was based on a thousand lies. I will give you an example. The Bible is supposed to be the word or God or at least words inspired by God but the Bible says that God fixed the earth upon its foundations not to be moved forever. But scientists have known for a very long time that the earth does move. So that fact shows the Bible is incorrect about the earth. So perhaps it is incorrect about the existence of God. The Bible says repeatedly that God created the earth and stars, the sun and moon, the seas and mountains, the plants and animals. But in all these things where is God to be found? Nowhere because they say he is invisible. So I see no reason to believe he created anything of the world and will not believe in Him until He reveals himself to me. No, I will believe in only in the things of nature and believe they came to be in the way science explains because that is one thing the Bible never explains is how God created these the things of the world.

"'There is a psalm in the Bible that says that God sends *"forth springs into the watercourses that wind among the mountains, and give drink to every beast of the field, till the wild asses quench their thirst."* But if you follow the rivers and springs you will not find God. We know the ocean gives its water to the clouds that carry it to the mountaintops and that it is that water that becomes the streams that flow into rivers. It is not God who waters the earth but the oceans, clouds, and rain. And the Bible says God raises grass for both men and animals but any farmer knows that it is not God but the seeds of plants that provide grass for men and animals. It says that God planted the cedars of Lebanon but no one has ever seen God plant a single tree but I have seen the people of my village plant many fruit trees. And they not the Lord water and care for those trees. The psalm also says God made the moon. But the idea is silly. How did God make the moon? In the way your mother makes meatballs for her *albóndigas* soup? You see it makes no sense. And there are a billion billion moons in the Universe of which only a few can be seen. Why did God make so many? Because he didn't. Science tells us the moon formed when the earth was struck by a giant object as it was forming and the material that flew from the earth were join together by gravity to create the giant rock in the sky we call the moon..."

"'That's a very strange story of how the moon came to be.'

"'It is but less strange than the moon having been made by a ghost with no hands. That is the problem with the Bible. It wants us to believe that which no one has ever seen. This psalm also says "How manifold are your works, O Lord!" But what sense does that make when no one has ever seen the Lord making anything. Yet we see everyday what nature makes and causes to happen.'

"'I think understand but it is very strange because I never questioned that the world was made by God. Yet, as you say, I have never seen God. And when I prayed to God the only response was silence. So I think I understand. You are truly wise, Papa, to know such things.'

"'If I am wise it is because I have learned from others. The man I learned this from was a very strange philosopher with a very big moustache...'

"'Like that of Pancho Villa?'

"'No, much larger. The philosopher is Nietzsche and his writings are very strange. But wise I think because like Darwin he understood that human are just animals and that life is a struggle but unlike Darwin he thought struggle was good because it made people strong. He did not like the religion of the Jews because he understood it was all lies and gave credit to God for people's happiness when they themselves deserved credit for their success in life. And it made people feel that they were sinners if misfortune struck when in truth they did nothing wrong. And it is true. In the Old Testament the Jews can never please God. All he does is complain even though no people in the ancient world was more devoted to their God. Nietzsche like Christianity even less which is in fact also a Jewish religion. He disliked it because unlike the old Jewish religion it celebrates weakness and hates life...'

"'Christianity hates life? I thought Jesus was love."

"'He was but he loved only God. He did not love this world. He thought this world was a place of sin and all he talked about was God and the spirit and heaven. At least the old Jews had some love for this world even if they give God all the credit. But the Christian Jews rejected the world as a place of sin, a place to escape from. But what are those things Christians talk about so much—God, spirit, angels, the Devil, heaven and hell? Who has seen any of them? No one except those people in the Bible and those who have been brainwashed by the Church as Juan Diego was. And he is a good example of how Christianity is life-denying as the philosopher says. After he and his wife were baptized they stopped having sex...'

"'It is very strange that a man and wife living together would not have sex.'

"It is not only very strange but unnatural. And that tells you the man was brainwashed by the fathers of the Church who are also unnatural men. So one hears about people talking to God or the Virgin or witnessing miracles but I have never met a person who saw an angel or the Virgin or witnessed a miracle just as I have never seen a flying saucer or know anyone who has. And who knows perhaps there are aliens living elsewhere in the Universe but I will not believe in them until I see them. Why is there, Lope, so much talk about God, Jesus, angels, and Devils but none to be seen. Supposedly they all still exist and everywhere are influencing the world but they are nowhere to be found...'

"'And it that what you learned from the philosopher Nietzsche?'

"'From him and others. But most important these men taught me to think for myself and not just accept what I am told by priests and the Bible or anyone. What they say is believe in what you see, hear, and feel. Don't be told what to believe. I was just amazed at what Nietzsche said as you are. He said that Christianity has not even a single point of contact with reality...'"

"'I don't understand, Papa.'

"'I did not myself understand at first. What the philosopher says is difficult to comprehend and I will tell you why, something else that I learned from the philosopher. We've all been brainwashed. I too once believed the vision of Juan Diego because I too believed as he did because I had been brainwashed by the Church...'

"'Then the whole village is brainwashed.'

"'Yes but that does not matter. Nietzsche once said the truth is not for everyone.'

"'Like women and children.'

"'Yes. But let me explain what I found so difficult at first to understand. Nietzsche said that the Bible and Church would have us believe in imaginary causes such as God and the soul, that God created the Universe, the earth, the sky, the seas, and all of life. In that way he would be the cause of everything. But he isn't because he does not exist. If he existed he could hear us talking at this moment and send an angel to show us that what I am saying is wrong. But doesn't even though the Church says that he would rather say nothing and have me and you burn in hell. I don't believe a god who created everything would be so petty. The Bible and the Church would also have us believe in a false story about the purpose of the world. That it was created by God for human beings. But then God became tired of everyone except the Jews his chosen people to whom he gave the land of the Canaanites. And then God appeared as Jesus to warn everyone one that they better believe in him because the world will end with Judgment Day which is when he will decide who will spend eternity in heaven or in hell. You see the Bible and the Church would have everyone believe that is the true story of the world—the purpose of the Universe and the reason why we are here.'"

"'But it is just make-believe is what the philosopher is saying.'

"'Not Just Nietzsche but many great philosophers and scientists. What angered Nietzsche was that the teachings of the Bible and the Church which represents the Bible caused people to disrespect nature and life. It isn't just a lie but a hateful lie. At one time people believed the world was flat but that was no fault of their own. And once it was proven that it was not flat they changed their thinking. What the Bible and Church teach is that all people are sinners and the world is an evil place because it is a place of temptation, that all natural desires are evil. Christians hate the body because it is through the body that we enjoy life—the pleasures of food, drink, sex, and many more pleasures. And as we enjoy life we forget about God and the Church because they are of no use to us. So they make up the lie that if we do not believe and obey the Bible and the Church we will burn in hell. You see, Lope, without the carrot of heaven and the stick of hell God is of no use to us. Everything we desire the earth, nature, and other people provide.'

"'But people don't want to die and be no more.'

"'That is the great fear that the Bible and the Church put into people's minds. There was a time when people accepted that this life is a gift to be enjoyed and then is no more. That is one way Nietzsche said that Christianity turned people into cowards. All other creatures must accept death as the end of their existence. But Christianity says no. We do not have to accept death...'

"'But, Papa, don't you fear death?'

"'Not today. I may fear it when I'm old but if I do I will also accept it. And I will not call in a priest to hear my confession and administer last rites. I will die like the creatures of the fields. And I will die grateful that I found you again and that I was a *soldado* for my country and people.'

"'And these lies why were they made up. Was it just because people were afraid?'

"'People have always been afraid just as animals are often afraid. So they created gods to be their powerful allies. The pagans prayed to the gods to help them in every way—to keep their families and people safe, to make their crops grow, to give them victory in war. For each important thing that people depended on a god was invented. And originally it was the same for the Jews. But then they came up with the big idea that they were special for one reason alone. And that was because they had been chosen as the people for the most powerful God..."

"'Because they were inferior to other peoples.'

"'You remember, very good. Yes they were an insignificant group of tribes of which there were many even as there are today in places such as Africa and South America even Mexico. But the Jews could not accept their insignificance but could do nothing about it in the real world. So they invented a make-believe world, one in which they were the most important people. But even though they thought of themselves as God's chosen people nothing really changed. They were still bullied. So what difference did God make in this world? That's when some Jews came up with the idea that this world was unimportant. That God had this big plan for them in the next world, a much better world called heaven...'

"'The Jews who believed in Jesus?'

"'And others. The idea was not invented by Jesus. He learned it from other Jews perhaps the Essenes or Pharisees. Both believed in a life after death and that God had a bigger plan for his people because things were going very bad. The Jews were under the control of the Romans and the Romans would soon destroy Jerusalem and the Jewish temple. So they had to believe that either God didn't really care about them or that he had something else in mind. And that is how Christianity was born. The focus shifted from this world to the next. This world was rejected so failure in it did not matter. It was the greatest lie ever told but it had great appeal to people like the Jews who were nobodies but especially those who had been defeated by life. As you know for most people life is hard. Those were the people Jesus preached to. Telling them that they were the people most special to God, not the rich and successful but the poor and unsuccessful."

"'And that was a lie?'

"'Yes a very pleasant lie, a lie Jesus wanted to believe himself because he was a very ordinary man, a carpenter. Isn't that why the nobodies like him because he was one of them. He suffered. That is why Nietzsche disliked Christianity so much because it's hero is a loser.'

"'Jesus was a Loser?'

"'Tell me, Lope, if Jesus was not the son of God then what was he?'

"'A carpenter and a preacher.'

"'And if he was not the son of God and if his God Yahweh was just an invention of his people then what did he really accomplish.'

"'That would mean he was simply a storyteller.'

"'Or worse *un estafador*, a con artist who lived off other people by telling them lies. In that way he was like the priest of every village. Tell me what does the priest do?'

"'He talks about the Bible, baptizes people, marries them and buries them.'

"'That is correct. All he does is talk. He talks about the stories in the Bible which are mostly not true. He baptizes people, mostly babies, and for what purpose? It is a rite of initiation. They become members of the Christian cartel before they have a chance to think about what it is they are joining just as their parents had before them. Then they go to church. In a way baptism is a net used to catch fish. And once caught it is very difficult for the fish to escape. But the Church's net is words and what is caught are people. The priest says words that not long ago the people did not even understand because they were spoken in Latin. And while he speaks he sprinkles holy water on the baby. And why is the water holy and has magical powers? Because the priest asked God to bless it. But the water does not change. In fact it is well known that water that has been blessed can still have germs and viruses in it. So how can such water be holy? It is holy only in the mind of the believer who has been tricked into thinking so by the words of the priest. Supposedly the rite of baptism delivers the person from sin, death, and the devil and enables him to enter into the kingdom of Christ and live with him forever. But those are only words. People still sin and die. What does it mean really to enter into the kingdom of Christ. It is supposed to mean that one receives a ticket that will allow him to go to heaven and by doing so avoid going to hell. But off course no one knows anything of heaven or hell...'

"'But the Church helps the poor.'

"'Yes it does which is not a bad thing. But that is the only real thing the Church does for people but to do that it uses money taken from people who truly work for a living, people who grow our food, build all the things we use in life, who recue us when we are in danger, who treat us when we are sick. These are real things. And today we have social workers who help the poor. But really what the Church is about is itself. It is a very rich and powerful institution that lives off the sweat of working people. The priests are not like you and me. We must work like animals to survive. Priests and nuns are people who hide from life. Once they join the Church they will have a place to live, clothes to wear, food to eat, and they cannot be fired, not even priests who fondle children. And who makes such a life possible? I will tell you. Working people, people who were initiated before they could think for themselves, who were promised pie in the sky which they became addicted to because after the promise was made they could no longer face death without the promise of another life. Christianity is a drug and like all drugs it appeals most to the people who have least. But you and I are animals like the lion and the eagle. We struggle in the world, we fight to survive, and we will accept life and death for what they are because we are not cowards.'

"'So, Papa, is that all religion is, a lie?'

"'Religion has always been make-believe but this is not a lie. Whoever Jesus was and there is no way of knowing who he was because the Jesus of the Bible is a character in a story just like the characters in the stories the Greek poet Homer wrote...'

"'I do not know him.'

"'No but you shall. His stories are important because they are make-believe but still true to life. They are not pie-in-sky stories but about the struggle to survive and the importance of one's people. There are gods but mostly they are symbols of the good and bad things that are of this world. But I don't believe Jesus was a liar because he believed what he spoke of was true. But those who used Jesus to control others were liars. They used Jesus to acquire power over others. And the greatest liar of all was Saint Paul. He was an educated Jew. You remember I told you that the Jews were jealous of the great civilizations such as those of the Egyptians, Babylonians, and Romans. They mock them in their Bible and pretended the Jews were the greatest people in the world. Yet everywhere the Jews look they were reminded of their failure. Nietzsche said what they felt was resentment which is hatred cause by jealousy and envy. It was Saint Paul who realized that being God's people didn't make any difference. It was a kind of escape from reality. When he lived the Jews were controlled by the Romans. And then he had his big idea...'

"'A vision of Jesus that knocked him to the ground' said Lope who wanted to show his father that he too knew things.

"'You know the story. That is very good, Lope because it means that you will become wise. Yes. He never knew Jesus or anyone who had. He lived in the city of Tarsus which was very far from Jerusalem. He was brought up a Jew but had been educated as a Roman citizen. So he understood very well the pagans he hated because he was a Jew fill with resentment. The vision he had probably never happened but was invented by himself. But he did have another vision which was how Jesus could be used to defeat not only the Romans but all pagans. Defeat them by Judaizing them not with the old Judaism which was not possible because it did not accept pagans but despised them. But the Judaism of Jesus could be used to accept pagans and by doing so destroying them just as the Church has been destroying pagans for two thousand years. You remember the story of Juan Diego?'

"'I do, Papa. He saw the Virgin.'

"'Yes but there is more to the story. Originally Juan was a pagan and his name was Cuauhtlatoatzin which means talking eagle in the Nahuatl language the language of our people. You see when the priests converted Cuauhtlatoatzin they destroyed him, changing him from a pagan to a Christian. That is why they gave him a new name, a Christian name, to show that Cuauhtlatoatzin was no more. And tell me, Lope, how many men do you know who have the name *Jesús*?'

"'Very many.'

"'Yes, and so Cuauhtlatoatzin was destroyed. And then the Church made him a saint and why would they do that? I will tell you. Because soon after his conversations with the Virgin and his having received roses from her in the middle of winter which he showed to the Bishop Zumárraga word spread and within seven years the Indian people, the Mexican pagans, accepted the Spaniards and eight million converted to the Catholic faith. And Juan Diego was very much like Jesus. No one knows what happened. The story of Juan Diego was written by the priest Miguel Sánchez more than a hundred years after the miraculous events were supposed to have happened. There is no record of the visions and miracles. Bishop Zumárraga said and wrote nothing about the miracles or Juan Diego. Miguel Sánchez was priest storyteller. Today we would call what he wrote propaganda. He was the one who made Diego into a saint. That is what Saint Paul did with Jesus. He made him into something he was not originally and he did this as a way of getting revenge against the pagans...'"

"'But then they lied.'

"'Of course. But that did not matter. The truth does not matter. You see a lie is simply a tool that can be used in many ways. The Jews accepted the lie of their faith because it made them feel important. The same is true of Juan Diego who was only a farmer and maker of mats. He was a nobody and the Church told him he could become an important somebody if he became a Christian—a favorite of God who would allow him to live forever in paradise. How could a poor man resist. It was a beautiful lie. The Church uses lies as a way of acquiring power over people who then keep the Church in business. But Saint Paul used lies as a weapon against the pagans he hated. He would destroy them by Judaizing them...'"

"'*Judaizing* that is a strange word. I do not think I understand.'

"'Who are the Jews, Lope?'

"'Jews are the people who worship the God of the Bible but not Jesus.'

"'That is correct. What God do Christians worship?'

"'The same.'

"'Exactly. So Christians are also Jews. And it is true that today Jews do not worship Jesus as a God but who wrote the New Testament which says Jesus is the son of God?'

"'I am not sure. Were they Jews?'

"'Yes. They were all Jews. And what of Jesus?'

"'He is a Jew as well. I think I understand now. Christians do not think they are Jews but they are because they worship a Jewish god and a Jewish man they believe is God. And you say that is what Saint Paul wanted to do—to destroy the pagans who the Jews despised.'

"'It is called Saint Paul's revenge. He used the story of Jesus, which was mostly invented, as a weapon to destroy the pagans. Not only to destroy the pagans but to make the Jews the most important people in the world. And he was very successful. Christian churches are everywhere in the world and the people who worship in them worship the god of the Jews, the Jewish man-god, Jesus, and even a Jewish mother, Mary, as Juan Diego did. He gave up his goddess Tonantzin a goddess of the earth to worship the Jewish mother of a Jewish god. That is how the Jews killed the gods of the earth, most important mother nature. That is how they got the pagans to forget about the earth and all of her good things, even to despise her, and to think only of things not of this world, to love a god who is nowhere to be found, to love his son who is nowhere to be found, and to love his mother who has nothing to do with the lives of the people.'

"'So it's all a lie.'

"'The truth is that it is all a lie, yes. And that is why the Church has prevented for centuries people thinking for themselves, why it has tortured and murder those who disagreed with its teachings, why it has burned the books of thinkers who disagreed with its teaching. What do you think the Church would have done to Nietzsche had he been born when the Church was all powerful?'

"'They would have tortured and killed him and burned his books.'

"'Yes, and they would have been condemned as *un anticristo*.'

"'*Un anticristo!* Is that not very bad?'

"'That is what the Church wants everyone to believe. But Nietzsche was simply a free-thinking philosopher who believed that Christianity is a myth like all the other myths about gods. But he believed Christianity is different from the others because it is a myth that hates life, hates reality, hates the truth, celebrates suffering, and turns people into *niños asustados*. He is an antichrist only in that he is against Christianity.'

"'Still I can see why the Church would hate this philosopher.'

"'But is it not strange, Lope, that this philosopher was doing only what the Church has done for two-thousand years—converting people's thinking about what is true and not true. Except Nietzsche would not torture and kill those who disagree with him. He would not burn their books. As a philosopher he would only say prove to me that what I say is false...'

"'And this most dangerous book of his, what is it call?'

"'It is called *The Antichrist.*'

"'Yes, of course. I must read it someday.'

"'You will read many books, Lope. To do so is a great adventure.'

"'But isn't it a sad thing.'

"'That the Christian story is not true? No. You know, Lope, some lies are good and harmless. We allow children to believe in Santa Claus because it is a fairytale that brings them joy. But the Christian story has brought much harm and the joy it promises is a lie. The gifts children receive from Santa are real. And when they are older we tell them that Santa is only make-believe. And when we do perhaps we tell them that make-believe is only for children and that adults who continue to believe in such stories are not are not adults at all but only children.

"'But you said it is acceptable for women to believe such things.'

"'We allow women to believe what they wish if it makes them happy. There is nothing worse than an unhappy woman. But a man cannot be both child and a man.'

"'And what of us, Papa? If Christianity is a lie then is it not true that we are not so important? We are just ordinary people.'

"'Being important is not what is most important in life. The greatest value of life is in the everyday living of it. That is what the Church has denied. That is why Nietzsche hated the lie of the Church because it turned people from that which is most valuable in life—the living of everyday—the work we do, the food and drink we consume, the pleasure of making love and having children to love and care for, the enjoyment of nature and our neighbors, and serving our people.'

"'But the Mexican people are not so important either.'

"'They are not a great people as the Greeks and Romans were. And they are not great in the way America is with its technology and big military. In truth America is not a great nation but only a powerful one. But greatness is not what life is about. In fact the pursuit of greatness has been the biggest source of human suffering. The Germans, Japanese, and Italians wanted to be great and by doing so caused the greatest war in history. War is what comes most often from the pursuit of greatness because men who wish to be great have used war to do so. Which means they kill millions of their own people and others so that they will be remembered—like Alexander the Great or Napoleon or Hitler or today George Bush.

"'America has put men on the moon, a most difficult thing to do. But what does it mean? Nothing. Has that made people happier? Perhaps the people at NASA but no one else. Most people liked the moon as she was before the American astronauts visited her. And today she is covered with junk from many missions by many nations. She has been treated as a whore by men who love to play with their machines. And for what? I do not respect men who disrespect nature. They are like the scientist Frankenstein, whose greatness is foolishness. If a person wishes to be great then let him do so without harming others. Let him become a great artist or thinker such as Nietzsche. Or let him become great by helping his people in some way. But only fools pretend to be great when they are not.'

"'Like the Jews and the Christians.'

"'How is one to be great by simply believing he is? And that is all those religions do—make people believe they are great even though they have done nothing out of the ordinary. To be great people must accomplish something worthwhile something of real value that they have produced with their hands and minds. It is believed that Jesus was the greatest man who ever lived. But that is lie. He was a carpenter who spent his life preaching untruth. How is that great? But the men who are the least of men are the religious swindlers who believe they are God's anointed but who have accomplished nothing really worthwhile except to inspire millions into believing in a lie and even having them going off to war in the name of that lie. And what I say is true not only the Jews and Christians but of the Muslims as well, whose religion is also a Jewish faith. They are all make-believers and deceivers.'

"'And that is why you are not religious, Papa?'

"'I am a spiritual man—nature, my family, and my people are my religion. I am a godless pagan. You know Nietzsche did admire a little the religion of

Buddhism though I think he dislike all religions because he thought them to be false. But he hated most the ones that turned people away from life. Buddhism he said is a hundred times more realistic than Christianity. It accepts suffering but does not celebrate it as does Christianity whose hero was humiliated, whipped, stabbed, and nailed to a cross. That is why Christian martyrs were so willing to be tortured and fed to the lions, why they mortified the flesh, which means to kill the flesh, by punishing their bodies by whipping, piercing, and cutting them, or by denying themselves the pleasures of food, drink, and sex, or by living as beggars.

"'That is why Juan Diego and his wife gave up sex after they became Christians and why after her death he lived like a hermit which is very unnatural for a Mexican to do. They did these things because they wanted to suffer like Jesus. Such a religion celebrates that which is unnatural and unhealthy. Buddhism is more restrained and perhaps the most honest of all religions because it doesn't believe in God or pie in the sky. The Buddhist accepts life as it is and enjoys what it offers. He teaches like the Greek wise men, the Stoics and Epicureans, that life should be lived in moderation. He resents no one and does not try to convert others to his faith. He seeks most of all to live in peace. You have seen the Buddha haven't you Lope?'

"'You mean the smiling fat man?'

"'Yes, and is he happy?'

"'He's very happy but I think he is not so moderate in his eating.'

"'That is simply to show that enjoys life. But how does he differ from Jesus on the cross?'

"'Jesus suffers.'

"'Yes, and all the women below, the three Marys, are very sad. The idea is life is a very sad affair because people are sinners. It's because people are sinners that Jesus was crucified. He died for all the sinners in the world. And sin is a very important idea in Christianity but there no sin in Buddhism. The Buddhist believes people can be foolish and stupid or they can be wise. But the ones who are not wise are not sinners. And there is no God to hate them when they are foolish and stupid. God does not have to punish foolish and stupid people because most likely they will be punished by what comes of their foolishness and stupidity.'

"'I find it strange that the Buddhists do not believe in sin. I thought everyone did.'

"'I tell you something that you will find very surprising. Sin was invented by the Jews but it was the Jew Saint Paul who used it as a weapon.'

"'Do you remember what I said Saint Paul wanted to accomplish?'

"'To destroy the pagans by making them into Jews, which still sounds very strange to me.'

"'A person who worships the Jewish god and a Jewish man as if he were a god is no longer a pagan. He is a Jew.'

"'Yes, I understand. It's just the idea is strange to me.'

"'There is a saying that truth is stranger than fiction and I believe it. But making a man believe he is a sinner is not enough to make him change his faith. Something more is needed. Tell me, Lope, what happens to sinners?

"'They go to hell.'

"'But not all of them.'

"'No, not those... I see. A sinner can avoid going to hell by becoming a Christian and going to church.'

"'Very good. So you see how Saint Paul and the Catholic Church frightened people into becoming Christians. That was the Jews' victory over the pagans and how the Church became wealthy and powerful. But really, who truly knows about hell?'

"'The Church.'

"'That is what the Church would have everyone believe. But the Church doesn't know. No one knows. But it was an idea that Saint Paul who really is no saint at all and the Church used to convert the pagans. But again something more was needed, and that was the idea that everyone is a sinner not just those who do bad things. And of course that is a lie...'

"'Because there are people who do only good.'

"'Yes. There are such people even in the Bible. Do you know of the story of Job?'

"'He was a man who suffered but that is all I know.'

"'He was a good man who never sinned but God allowed Satan to cause Job great suffering because Satan said that if Job suffered enough he would reject God for being unjust which he was for playing this little game.'

"'You mean God allowed Satan to torture Job to make him say what he normally would not say.'

"'That is true, Lope. But Job would not speak against God. He desired only to argue his case with God because he thought his punishment was undeserved. And that was another thing Nietzsche hated about the religion of the Jews. It made people who failed in life feel like sinners even though they were not sinners but only unfortunate. But, Lope, do you know why it was important to make all people think they were sinners?'

"'I think I do, Papa. If people believe they are sinners then they will fear going to hell so they become Christians to avoid going to hell. But as you say not everyone is a sinner. There are many bad people in the village but there are also many good people. That part I don't understand.'

"'It is nothing to be ashamed of. When I was your age I knew none of these things. I had to learn the truth and so will you. And I see that you are a very fast learner which makes me very proud because I see you are my son. But it is true that not everyone has sinned. So the Church invented Original Sin...'

"'The sin that came from Adam and Eve.'

"'See! You are a very smart boy. Yes. Saint Paul said, "*Therefore, as through one man sin entered into the world, and death through sin; and so death passed unto all men, for that all sinned.*" And that one man was Adam...'

"'But Eve sinned as well.'

"'Yes but at the time it was believed that the man passes on the human seed and the woman is like the soil in which the seed grows. And if the soil was unclean in some way then the seed grew into a misshapen person. But then people knew nothing about genetics. And what is strange is why an all-knowing God would not tell his people the truth about such things. So what Saint Paul said was "*through one trespass the judgment came unto all men to condemnation*" meaning all people were sinners because of Adam and were bound to go to hell. But they could be saved if they accepted Jesus Christ as their Lord and Savior. So what are people like Juan Diego going to do?'

"'Become Christians.'

"'Become Jews by worshiping a Jewish god and turning their lives over to a Jewish man, Jesus. Saint Paul won his victory over the pagans and the Church became rich.'

"'And everyone was convinced that what Paul said was true?'

"'No. The people who were educated and wise or who were happy with their own religion were not convinced. But once the Jewish religion became the religion of the Romans people had no choice. The pagan gods were declared demons and those who worshiped them could be tortured and put to death. And the schools of the philosophers and scientists were closed and their books burned. Then people had no choice but to worship the Jewish god and the Jewish god-man. And after many centuries people had become brainwashed and believed the lie was true. And they wanted it to be true because now they were afraid of death and wanted to be able to call on Jesus and Mary when life was difficult because of poverty or disease.'

"'I see why Nietzsche believed the truth is not for everyone. I myself find it hard to accept.'

"'But you will accept it because you are a man and not a child. And we will let the women and children believe the lie because they are not men. That was what Nietzsche disliked about Christianity. It made women of men.'

"'And, Papa, are you a Buddhist?'

"'No, Lope. I'm just a man and that is enough for me.'

"'I think you are a very brave man to accept such a truth.'

"'Would it be better for me to accept the lie because I was afraid?'

"'No, of course not.'

"'Besides, now there are medicines for sadness so perhaps there is no longer any reason to be a coward hiding from the truth. I do not want to be one who runs from the truth, Lope. We are truth seekers you and I. It's in our blood. That is why I have sought to be like your great-grandfather who was a brave man who sought the truth even in the Bible. And what he learned in his reading of it was that the world and the men who live in it are imperfect. It is the same in Señor Darwin's book *Origin of Species*. The world is a desperate place where every living thing struggles to survive and that is the story found in the Old Testament, struggle and war. But Señor Darwin's book is more honest because there is no God to help, no punishment awaiting evil men or reward awaiting good men. Just death... struggle and death.'

"'Hmm, I can see why the gringos do not like this man who speaks the truth. His truth is very unfriendly. I am not sure I like it either.'

"'No they do not but that is to our advantage, Lope, because while they pray to their God to help them and look forward to going to heaven we shall take back our homeland. And you are correct when you say the truth is unfriendly but it will be a greater friend to us, *mijo*, than the lies will be to the *sopaipillas* people.'

"'You truly do not like the gringos do you, Papa?'

"'No, Lope, I do not and you will see why when we get to America. It is difficult to like a people who have become and perhaps always were consuming stomachs always half empty and half full of *mierda*. I would not call them the *sopaipillas* people but *gente del vientre* but Señor Lopez was right too because like *sopaipillas* the gringo is also full of hot air.'

"And, Señor Thomas, Arsenio went on again about how the stomachs of the gringo grow larger each day. That is why we sometimes call you gringos *gabachos* instead of *gringos*. The word once meant the French but now means the gringo as taker, pillager, plunderer, thief, consumer, and glutton. And Arsenio warned Lope that he must always be on his guard against the *gabacho* soul thieves. He said that Lope can rob the *gabacho* thief and kill the *gabacho* murderer but that he must keep the spirit of his people in his heart. 'If you forget that you are a *mejicano*,' he said, 'the gabacho will cease to be a dragon and will become a whirlwind that will swallow you as the leviathan swallowed Jonah.'

"Lope was now very confused because what he had known of the gringos was what he had seen in the movies."

"'But, Papa, you say that the gringos believe in a false religion, the religion of Jesus. Still does this mean that none of them are good people? I know you do not like Señor Bush and nobody does in Mexico because of his evil war but still all gringos cannot be so bad.'

"'Remember, Lope, that it was the gringo Christians who supported *el presidente* even after he began his evil war.'

"'Yes, that is true, Papa.'

"'Perhaps there are a few good gringos, Lope, just as there are a few good priests but America is like a body infected with cancer. Some cells will not be infected by the cancer but the body will remain mortally ill and will eventually die. And I do not believe so very many good cells exist because the spirituality of the gringo is mostly for show like the gringo priests who wear the clothes of holy men but violate the little children who come to them for guidance. The gringos have worn masquerades for so long they are unable tell the real from the false. They are a sick people but do not see their sickness even though their bodies are covered with sores. They have forgotten what it is to be healthy.

"'General Gonzales would say the reality of the *gabacho* is his masquerade. In that way America has become like its Hollywood—a nation of actors and directors and make-believe stories. Everything in America is phony—except the phoniness itself. That is real. Again you can see what America is in *Presidente* Bush. He talks about his religion but he thinks only of money and power. In that way he is like the *Judíos* who talk of God but live for money, like Jack Abramoff who sought not to do good things for America but only to get rich. Perhaps in his mind being a Jew means that the nonJews are nothing because they are not favored by God though the Jews do not seem to have been favored by God either. So with the help of the gringos the Jews stole Palestine from the Palestinians all the while speaking of themselves as God's very own people the holiest of all people. Señor Bush is a phony, a phony man of God, a phony student, a phony *vaquero*, a phony soldier, and now he conducts a phony war though the deaths are not phony. They are real.'

"'So none of the gringos are true Christians. Is such a thing possible, Papa?'

"'What does it mean to be a true Christian anyway, Lope? How can something that is false ever be true? Besides even when everyone believed it was true it made no difference. The Christians have always preached peace and meekness and forgiveness as they conquered the world. Did not the Spanish conquer Mexico? Why is it that the languages of North and South America are English and Spanish and Portuguese in Brazil?'

"'Because the Europeans came and conquered those places.'

"'Yes, Lope, but they also came as Christians to conquer the hundreds of tribes of Indians, taking their lands and destroying their cultures and their languages. It is from Christianity that comes the gringo's *melting pot* idea. The Christians have tried to melt all the religions of the world in the great Christian melting pot. And today they continue their destruction. Their missionaries scour the world like army ants seeking out the poor who are Buddhist or Moslem or some African faith and converting them with lies of God's love and future prosperity...."

"Like the Mormons who come to our village, always two boys wearing suits and riding bicycles."

"Exactly. They are lying gringos proselytizers who told American Indians the lie that their ancestors were Jews who sailed from Jerusalem to the New World six-hundred years before Christ. And of course an Indian who became a Mormon was no longer an Indian. What he became was nothing. And now the Mormons have replaced the Spanish priests and English missionaries spreading lies for the sake of money and power.

"'And the gringos did the same with their Marxism, a godless religion also inspired by a Jew. The Marxist communists wanted to melt all the cultures of the world into one melting pot, the Marxist state. It was like wanting take all the colors from the rainbow and replace them with one color that was not beautiful, so all the world would be various shades of

Marxist gray. Do you see why it is impossible for me to like the gringo, Lope?'

"'I understand, Papa.'

"'But our leaders will use Christianity to our favor, like the late great Father Luis Olivares who declared his L.A. parish a sanctuary for millions of illegal immigrants. Like all Latinos he disregarded the *migra*, hated the FBI, used the gringo laws and courts when they were useful and ignored them when they were not, mocked the gringo politicos and bureaucrats, and scolded the gringo priests who did not embrace illegal immigrants.

"'He also used the Bible as a sword against our gringo enemies saying to them, "Has the gringo forgotten the Lord God's words to Moses? God said *'When an alien resides with you in your land, you shall not oppress the alien. The alien who resides with you shall be to you as the citizen among you; you shall love the alien as yourself, for you were aliens in the land of Egypt: I am the LORD your God.'"* So you can see how wise a man the padre was confounding the gringo Christians with a whirlwind of words just as the Jews had done before so that when they looked up they saw what was below and when they looked down they saw what was above.

"'Even the good padre's ghost continues the struggle to ensure that illegal immigrants shall remain in America with all the rights and privileges of any American citizen. I believe his ghost has recently frightened even Cardinal Mahony who is the big *jefe* in the Catholic Church in L.A. He once fought against us but now he pledges to defy immigration laws. I think that Father Olivares' ghost came to the Cardinal one night during a bad dream about pedophilia and whispered in his ear, "Do not forget, Your Holiness, the five million parishioners in your archdiocese who speak Spanish. And each Sunday do not forget which side of the wafer you ingest is buttered on. It is buttered on the brown side." And so now the great gringo priest is our priest a pocket priest. Was not Father Olivares a very wise man, Lope, a man who served God in order to serve his people?'

"'Yes, Papa, I see that he was very wise and I would like very much one day to go to the church where he preached.'

"'You shall, Lope. I will take you there myself for I have been there many times mostly to be among a gathering of our people. And though I am not a believer in the way of others I have learned from Father Olivares who perhaps learned it from Saint Paul that Christianity can work in mysterious ways to become a sword for those who understand it.'

"'And this man Mahony are not the gringos upset with him?'

"'No because they trust him as Jesus trusted Judas though as I have said Judas served Jesus but Cardinal Mahony does not serve the gringos but his own ambition as he did when he protected pedophilic priests. The Catholic Church serves itself as it did when it helped resettle thousands of Vietnamese in New Orleans East.

"'You see the gringos suffer from a religious sickness call *Adventism* which has clouded their minds as it has clouded the mind their *presidente*. America has become for the Christian gringos nothing but a place of waiting like a bus or train station. They believe they are living in what they call the *End Times* when Jesus will come again and they will be transported by God into heaven. For these Christians the *End Times* is a time of war which they call *Armageddon* and I think that is why the gringos are now in Iraq because the Adventists must have war and havoc in order to believe the end is near. But I will tell you this, Lope. What the *End Times* means to us is the end of the gringos. There is an Armageddon a battle between the good Latinos and the evil gringos and there will be a *rapture* a *carrying off* but it will be a *going off* of the gringos. And there will be a second coming but it will not be the Second Coming of Christ but of the Mexican people returning to the paradise of *Aztlán*. So as you can see, Lope, the *End Times* refers to the end of gringo time.'

"'That is very amazing, Papa. I see now that the world is a much stranger place than I thought.'

"'Only that the world is and that we are here is truly strange. But the living of life is not. It is in truth quite simple. So simple that the truth can be seen in the lives of the creatures who share the earth with us. The meaning of existence is simply to live and for humans to also be grateful. What is truly strange are those who wait for the chariot to come and take them to heaven. And while they have their eyes cast heavenward we the Mexican people who are rooted in the soil of the earth shall take back what the gringos stole from us because America is not an *estación de paso* for our people but our *destino*.'

"'And is what you say of the gringos also true of those my age? Will they not fight for their homeland?'

"'That is a very interesting and puzzling question, Lope. The few Americans who do turn out to protest the invasion of their country are always old never young. America's young people do not think like you. Most think only of themselves. Perhaps the thing most triste about the gringos is that their children have very little *patriotismo*. *La patria* does not exist for them.

They hate their towns and villages and move to the big cities where they can party. There they spend their time listening to rock n roll, rap, and reggaeton, taking drugs, decorating their bodies with bizarre tattoos, riding their skateboards or playing paintball or videogames. They are very much disengaged from reality like at their rave parties where they take the drug Ecstasy which allows them to dance all day and all night in a trance. Young people are the hope of every culture. That is why it is important for you to know these things. You are the future not me. America has no future because the minds of its youth are poisoned by the drugs the Mexican Mafia is quite willing to provide them because doing so makes them rich and the gringos weak.'

"'So the gringo youth will not fight us?'

"'To the contrary, Lope, were we to sneak across the border in the desert which we will not because I know of many other easier ways to enter the U.S. we would be greeted by gringo youths who would give us food and water and even take us to the hospital if we were sick. They call themselves *Volunteers for No More Deaths* and I am sure their work makes them feel good inside. Still, aiding the illegal aliens invading your country is an act of *traición*. They say what they do is a mission of mercy but I think it is a mission of suicide for America. But you see, I think these young people have no loyalty to America and are probably rich kids who are bored with nothing to do so they help those who do not like them and will one day destroy them.'

"'But what of the young people who fight in the wars?'

"'Yes, they would fight and die to protect their country but they are of no use against the millions of Mexicans invading their country because we come as civilians. That is just another example of our wisdom and the gringo's stupidity. And gringos have many other ways that could be used to stop us but they are too timid to use them. I will tell you the problem of the gringos. It is the same with the Europeans. They are too civilized. They are afraid to violate someone's human rights especially those of the civilians who enter their country illegally. They feel only pity. They even blame themselves for the invaders' poverty and hardship. They tell their police to leave the invaders be. And if their own patriots attack the invaders they not the invaders are arrested.

"'You see that is how we use America's civility and guilt against them. The Americans have become too much like Jesus who is perhaps their greatest source of guilt because he loved most of all the nobodies of the world which means that good Christians would also. He explained how a good Christian should behave, saying *"If someone strikes you on the right cheek, turn to him the other also. And if someone wants to sue you and take your tunic, let him have your cloak as well. If someone forces you to go one mile, go with him two miles. Give to the one who asks you, and do not turn away from the one who wants to borrow from you."* Jesus would not resist those who would take advantage of him. And you know how it turned out for him.'

'"He was crucified.'

'"Yes but he did not care because he was happy to return to heaven to live with his father, God. And many Americans wish to be like Jesus. So they turn the other cheek to the invaders and give them everything they need to survive in the country they have invaded. And as Jesus lost his life they will lose their country which was ours before and the Indians before us.'

'"Do all Americans feel guilty?'

'"No not all of them but enough mostly the Democrats. They feel guilty for the way America treated the Indians and black people. They feel guilty that America has great wealth. So what does their government do? Senator Ted Kennedy and President Johnson passed a law allowing millions more immigrants into the country. And even the Republican President Reagan gave amnesty to millions of illegal immigrants which was a very strange thing for a Republican to do because Republicans feel sorry for no one. But of course Reagan was thinking of cheap labor and wanted the economy to keep expanding. As I said before, the gringos are not very fertile.

'"But the best example of America's suicidal civility is the Fourteenth Amendment to the Constitution which says that any child born on American soil is American even if his parents are illegal aliens. And that is why all Mexicans try to have their children born in America even if they must return to Mexico because that way their children will have dual citizenship. So when they are older they can go to America as citizens and one day bring their parents to live in America as well. You know you have brothers and sisters in L.A. who are all American citizens even though their mother and I entered the country illegally. So we will be a big family and will look out for one another unlike the gringos who have forgotten the importance of family.

'"I do worry, Papa, that I am not a citizen.'

'"It is true you are not an American but do not worry. When the Democrats return to power and they will because President Bush is now known as America's worst president and the Republicans will have to pay.

Then the government will pass another amnesty and you and I and your mother and the *niños* will all be as American as the president. And soon the Hispanics will have enough control of the government to allow even more immigrants into America. Then America will no longer belong to the gringo. But that is what happens when a country becomes too civilized. It no longer will protect itself against invaders unless they are wearing military uniforms. It is very interesting that the Muslim attackers of 9-11 were civilians. And now because the Americans feel guilty for the killing and torture of so many Muslims they will allow millions of Muslims into the country to prove that they are truly a civilized people.'

'"I think the gringos are crazy.'

'"They are which is good for us.'

"Then Arsenio wish to speak again of the Greek poet Homer, about his hero Odysseus which Lope was now very interested in because his father said Homer's stories were important. But Lope was also sad, telling Arsenio that he felt stupid for knowing nothing of such a great man. Arsenio smiled and told him that he was not stupid.

'"It is not your fault Lope that you do not know the poet. Like me you grew up poor and uneducated. A man cannot be blamed for being poor if there is no work or uneducated if he is unable to go to school. But as I said before you soon will know about Homer and many other things besides because Americans will educate you even if you are illegal.' I could see what Arsenio said pleased Lope very much.

'"Being illegal,' Arsenio continued, 'doesn't really matter. It only means that you do not want to get caught committing a crime because then you will be sent back to Mexico but that does not matter either because you can return. The Mexicans in America are millions strong. We are already a nation within a nation. We are part of an even larger nation called the *Hispanic Nation* and we take care of our own because we have many organizations that protect us, organizations run by immigrants like us.

'"Let me give you an example. There is a Latina name Ann Marie Tallman. She is the granddaughter of migrants just like us and she is president of the Mexican American Legal Defense and Educational Fund, a national Latino civil rights organization that fights for the constitutional rights of illegal immigrants, which sounds very amazing to me since the Constitution is supposed to protect Americans but instead protects us. And there is Pablo Alvarado who is sometimes called the new Cesar Chavez. I don't believe that because this man is not a Mexican but he is a Latino and thus a part of the Hispanic Nation. He too entered America illegally and now fights for the rights of the *jornaleros* who also entered the country illegally.

"'And when the gringo threatens to send the *jornaleros* back to Mexico Pablo calls upon us to fill the streets in protest and we come by the thousands. And if the gringos and their politicians talk of deporting all of us who are in the country illegally which is now no longer possible Pablo's voice and voices of others will be magnified a million times by the Spanish-language radio deejays who will call the Latino faithful into the streets, like Eddie Tweety Bird Sotelo a really big voice on L.A. radio who also came to America illegally in the trunk of a car.

"'Then the gringo will find that he has awakened a leviathan and in the streets he will see not thousands but millions of Latinos waving thousands of Mexican flags and hundreds of American flags for the gringo media and even the red revolutionary flags with Che Guevara on them because he is an important symbol of the people's revolution. And the demonstrators will not be shouting *Sí, se puede,* "Yes, it can be done," but *Ya está hecho,* "It is done." And we will carry signs that declare *WE ARE AMERICA!* And the gringo will be able to do nothing because he is no more than Ahab was to the great whale Moby-Dick.'

"'I do not understand, Papa. A whale named Moby-Dick?'

"'Do not be ashamed, *mijo,* most gringos do not know the story of Captain Ahab and the great white whale even though it is their greatest novel and one that says much about the gringos themselves. They are an ignorant people like their *presidente,* preferring television to books. You shall not be though. I will not allow it. You shall read this and many other stories especially those of our own great novelists such as Mariano Azuela who is my favorite Mexican writer so that you might become wise. But for now you must listen to me as I tell you about the greatness of your people in America.

"'There is in America a very powerful organization called the ACLU an organization that has been compared to David in the Bible because it fights for the rights of aliens against the American Goliath and the American people who have often been called philistines. And its director is Anthony Romero. He is a Puerto Rican so you see, Lope, the Hispanic Nation within America is really many nations and so very powerful.

"'And as I have already explained, one of our own the son of Mexican immigrants Alberto R. Gonzales is the American Attorney General called the President's Counselor. Mr. Gonzales told immigration judges that he insisted that each immigrant *be treated with courtesy and respect.*" Those were his very words. So you know whose side he is on—it is ours. Is it not strange, Lope, that the American government arrests Iraqis who have done nothing against America other than fight for their homeland and then tortures them but treats *with courtesy and respect* those who invade America? The gringo is a mystery.'

"'Yes, truly, the gringo is *un misterio.'*

"'You know, Lope, that some people joke that the *R* in Señor Gonzales's name stands for Republican, but I think it stands for *reoccupation.* And who knows, the Attorney General could very well be the first Latino American *presidente.* And I will tell you this, after the first Latino *presidente* is elected there will be no more gringo presidents.'

"Having said this, Señor Thomas, Arsenio laughed and laughed while Lope and I looked on. We did not laugh but only stared at Arsenio who seemed very strange at that moment. It was then that I realized that I never really knew Arsenio though I had slept with him. Then he patted his son on the shoulder and said 'Lope, you must think your father is *loco* but he is not. I laugh with joy, with happiness, for how close our people have come to reclaiming their homeland. It's hard to believe how much power we have gained in just one generation. You know the story about the fox guarding the hen house well the American hen house has many clever Latino foxes in it and what do the gringos do? Nothing but sit and brood like a bunch of nervous fat hens. How can one not laugh at the gringo hens?

"'And who knows perhaps you will become a professor at a big American university in a Chicano Studies department where you will train other *soldados* and write propaganda that will inspire and lead young Latinos like yourself and confuse the gullible American gringos even more so that they will praise tolerance and condemn racism and bob their heads up and down in agreement like silly dolls. I know it sounds *loco* that Americans would educate the very people who seek to defeat them but, *mijo,* it is true.

"'Take for example Andrés Martinez. He comes from Chihuahua, Mexico, so he is a Mexican national just like you and me. I do not know about his parents but they probably came into the country illegally since most of the *nortemejicanos* either came illegally or their parents did. And what have the dimwitted gringos done for Martinez? They sent him to their most illustrious universities, Yale, Stanford, and Columbia so that he could become a most clever propagandist for the Latino people and now he is the Editor of the Editorial Page, which means the propaganda page, of the most prestigious newspaper west of the Delaware River, the *Los Angeles Times*, a newspaper that I believe will become bilingual in your lifetime and Hispanic in the life of your children. And I say this because on the editorial page there is an eagle with a sword and a quill, which is a pen made from a feather and each time I see that eagle do you know what eagle I see, *mijo?'*

"'Yes, Papa, the eagle of the Mexican people.'

"'I'm am certain, Lope, that one day you will be a great *soldado* in the *El Movimiento*; if not a great propagandist for the *mejicanos* like Andrés Martinez then perhaps a great *soldado* lawyer like Aaron Gonzalez who fights for the illegal workers in the South. Or Antonio Gonzalez, whose father was a Mexican immigrant and who is *un General* of a powerful political machine that organizes the Latinos to use their votes to overthrow the corrupt gringo like the communist leaders who once organized workers to defeat gringo America.

"'Or maybe you will become a great Chicano movie director like Robert Rodríguez whose movie *Sin City* laughs at the moral rot of gringo America. There are so many great Chicano and Chicana *soldados* fighting the American beast that has lost its soul like a powerful bull that is blind and must find its way with its nose. Again and again the great beast stumbles and falls and because it cannot see its way any longer one day comes to a cliff and tumbles over to its death. Our swords have been drawn against the serpent gringo so that we may free *Aztlán* but I will tell you something, Lope. Though we fight the gringo for *nuestra patria*, which he stole from us, and will never give up because our courage is like the steel of a samurai sword, the greatest enemy of the gringo is himself. In truth, gringos are *una gente enfermiza, una gente suicida*. So, my son, do you think you want to become one of *los Soldados Unidos por El Movimiento?'*

"'Very much,' said Lope, 'but I am still not so sure I am smart enough to be such a great man.'

"'Do not say such a thing' said Arsenio very seriously. 'You are my son, and look how much I have learned with only the mentoring of Señor Lopez and his books and of course with the counseling of your great-grandfather. You shall attend a very good high school a magnet school I think. The worst

American public schools are better than the best Mexican public schools and the magnet schools are the best of the American public schools. Your little brothers and sisters who you will soon meet began school at Benito Juárez Elementary School a very good school. It is strange that the school was named after Juárez a Mexican hero. He was a great Mexican patriot because he fought against the French. What the stupid gringos do not know is that he is a symbol of our fight against them because the gringos are now the *gabachos*. And believe me in the L.A. schools you see more Mexican flags than American flags.

"'Once with your brothers Aquiles and Ulises who I named after Homer's great heroes and with your sisters Victoria and Alejandra I attended a big ceremony at the school in honor of Juárez. That day the Mexican consul spoke in the school gym which was completely filled with hundreds of Mexican compatriots. Many of the children were waving Mexican flags but many also had small American flags tucked into their back pockets. This I did not quite understand and thought to be a little disrespectful. As you know, Lope, I do not respect the gringo but I believe we should not publicly disrespect the flag because doing so brings us no honor. When I said to Aquiles, who was sitting next to me, that I did not think sitting upon the American flag in public was a good thing he told me that the little flags were a symbol among the students that the Latinos have America in their pocket. Still I was not sure it was a good thing but said nothing more about it. Two days later the gringo school superintendent prohibited the flags and the ACLU stepped in saying that doing so violated the students' right to free speech. Then I had to laugh at the silly gringos who sometimes remind me of a dog chasing its tail.

"'After having said many good things about Juárez, the Mexican consul finished by saying, "*We will be the best for this country when we know our own roots.*" I understood that this statement was for the gringo press but I also understood that what he meant was that *this country will be ours once we have planted in its soil our Mexican roots.* And we plant those roots by changing names and putting up statues of Mexican patriots such as the statue of Juárez placed in a park in New York City. Then the school choir sang *Nuestro Himno* and it was very beautiful. Afterwards, your sister Victoria looked at me with tears in her eyes and said *"Papa, I like learning about Mexico because I'm Mexican."* What she said made me very proud and I told her that I was proud of her as I am proud of you, Lope, and to never forget that she is a Mexican not a gringo. But of course how can *un caballo* forget it is a horse and think it is a burro? No, such a thing is impossible.

"'Lope, I promise you that if you study hard the gringos will educate you and beg you to attend their best colleges so that you will become an educated *soldado, un soldado erudito en El Movimiento*. No, *mijo*, don't you worry about that. There are now thousands of *soldados eruditos* in the U.S. who were just as ignorant as you when they began their journey to *Aztlán*. And like many of them you shall study at a magnet school and become *un hombre erudito.*'

"'Magnet school! That sounds very strange, Papa.'

"'They are not so very strange but that the gringo would create such a thing is very strange."

"'Why is that, Papa?'

"'Because they were designed to destroy all-white gringo schools. They are another example of how the American government won't allow Gringos to live in their own communities. Gringos don't want their children going to schools that have minorities such as blacks and Hispanics because they believed the schools are dangerous and not so good which is true. That is how we create our barrios by having our gangs chase away the blacks and gringos. The gringos leave the neighborhoods with lots of minorities and create gringo communities in the suburbs so their children can go to all-white schools. But the government didn't want the gringos to have schools of their own so they started busing gringos back to the schools they had just left and busing blacks and Hispanics to the white schools. The gringos were very frustrated and I cannot blame because I do not want to live in a gringo neighborhood but in a barrio with my own people. And no one wants their children to be forced to go to school among strangers. So many gringos put their children in private schools. Then the government came up with the big idea of the magnet schools that are the best of public schools with special programs to attract students. That is what they should have done in the first place and forget about integrating the schools which is stupid. Black parents and Hispanic parents just want good schools for the children. They do not care that there are gringos in them. But governments are stupid and rarely listen to their people. They have big ideas of how their people should live and treat them like pieces of a game such as chess—pawns to be pushed this way and that.'

"'But I still don't understand why the call them magnet schools.'

"'Because they are supposed to attract students of all colors. The idea is to make a school that is like Disneyland where all the students—brown, black, yellow, and white—will want to go and will be happy and get along as people do at Disneyland. All the government cared about was mixing everybody together which is the idea of the melting pot. But we Mexicans will not be melted. In fact the blacks and the Asians won't be melted either. To be melted is to lose one's culture and soul.'

"'So it was a bad thing?'

"'It was a stupid idea for what it was supposed to achieve but it is good for us because you will go to such a school and there you will study hard. And we still live in our barrio. But no the magnet schools were not a big success because there were too few of them and the only gringos who came were those who could not afford to send their children to private schools. Why would they want to send their children to schools where they are hated by the other students especially the blacks and Hispanics who consider the honky gringos their enemy?

"'And though the magnet schools bring the black, Hispanic, Asian, and few white students together I know the students remain segregated among their own people. And of course the neighborhoods remained segregated as they should be because that is what people want. Even in the prisons inmates associate only with their own people. It is a law of life. And I ask you, Lope, why make a few very good schools just to mix people together and say that is a big success when many other schools are left forgotten? Why not make all schools very good? But as I said, the magnet schools are a big success for us because in L.A. most of the students in them are Latino.'

"'Does that mean the gringos no longer have schools of their own as we do in Mexico?'

"In L.A. that is true for the public schools.'

"'So it was not a good program for the gringos.'

"'You are more clever than you know, Lope. That is right. And is it not very strange that the government is most responsible for chasing the gringo from L.A.? Had it protected the borders and let the gringos be in their own communities then more would have stayed. Now there are very few gringos in L.A. It is complicated and I myself don't fully understand what happened. But one thing I do understand..."

"'That governments are not for their people but only for themselves,' interrupted Lope to show his father that he has been paying attention to his father's words.

"'Very good, Lope. Always they seek money and power for themselves and sometimes it is war they seek and sometimes they think they have a better idea of what their culture should be and so force the people to become this new thing such as fascists and communists did. In America the new idea is multiculturalism which means really to change America from a united nation to something like the United Nations. But a country of many nations will not be united. It is true all over the world even in Mexico that good governments are never good and bad governments are always bad. And in America the government has been very busy destroying gringo communities and schools. But what is bad for the gringo is good for us and when our people have reclaimed *Aztlán* we will not allow it to be destroyed. Why would a man build a house for his family one day and the next day set fire to it? Such a thing would be crazy but the gringo is *muy loco*.'

"'And where do the gringo students go when their schools become like the United Nations?'

"'Who knows? Who cares? They just go in search of a community like themselves. Of course the black students remain because unlike the gringos they are too poor to leave. I am very glad I am not a black person in America. They cannot leave the places they would like to leave and they are forced to leave the places they would like to remain in like New Orleans. But you need not worry about the black people—because you know who the majority is in the excellent magnet schools, yes?'

"'The Latinos' Lope said with a big smile.

"'That is right, my son. So you shall go to the very best high school at the gringo's expense and be with your own people. And we will not worry about the plight of the gringo. That is their job. We will worry only about our own people.'

"'That is very good, Papa. And I will study very hard and make you proud. Now, Papa, a while ago before you spoke of the Latino heroes in America and of the magnet school you were about to tell something more about the poet Homer who you named my brothers after. I am very interested in knowing about him because I can see he is important to you. But first, Papa, please explain to me the names of my brothers and sisters that I will soon come to know.'

"'Of course. Aquiles and Ulises are Homer's greatest heroes and great warriors. When your brothers were born I decided not to give them Christian names. I want to give them pagan names but names of fighter heroes who served their people. And your sisters too received such names. Victoria's name means victory because I know she will contribute to the victory of the Mexican people over the gringo. And I gave Alejandra a name that means warrior and defender because I know she too will serve her people.'

"'And my name, Papa?'

"'You, Lope, are named after the wolf, one of the most intelligent, brave, and loyal animals. He is an apex predator meaning he is a predator who has no predators of his own.'

"'Not even humans?'

"'Humans do not eat wolves but kill them for defense or fun. Those who kill wolves for fun with guns are cowards. I have no respect for such men. Unlike the eagle which is a magnificent animal the wolf is not a loner as people often believe. He mates for life, protects his territory, and serve his pack which is his family. So tell me, Lope, do you like your name.'

"'Very much.'

"I could tell, Señor Thomas, that Lope was pleased by what his father told him and it was at that moment I forgave in my heart Arsenio for Amancio's death which I then understood as something necessary if we were to do our part in helping the Mexican people to repossess *la patria* that the gringos stole from them. And I too decided then to be *una soldado* myself."

"Imelda, what do you mean you *forgave Arsenio for Amancio's death*?" I ask becoming alarmed. "Is there something about Arsenio that I don't know about but should?"

"That is what I am trying to tell you, Señor Thomas, but first I must finish what Arsenio wanted to tell Lope about Homer's story of Señor Odysseus who also sought to return to his own *Aztlán*."

"Jesus, Imelda, I'm more interested in what happened to your husband Amancio. I already know the story of Señor Odysseus."

Giving me a hurt look Imelda says, "Señor Thomas, I know you are an educated man but the way you understand the story may not be the same as Arsenio's and it might be good for you to know his understanding. Sometimes I think Arsenio is right that you gringos are very stupid. You don't see the writing on the wall because you do not take the time to do so."

"Okay, okay, Imelda, I'm listening. Finish about Señor Odysseus and I will try to be patient." Saying that, I glance warily at Arsenio whose broad smile seems to have grown more sinister.

"Pay attention to me, Señor Thomas, not to that donkey husband of mine."

"I'm paying attention, Imelda, but tell me one thing. Arsenio talks to Lope only about his grandfather. What about his parents?" The question sounded really Freudian but I was getting this creepy feeling about Arsenio and beginning to wonder whether he had experienced some childhood trauma that he doesn't want to talk about but turned him into some kind of psychopath that I'm now having to deal with.

"Lope once asked Arsenio about his father because, as you said, Arsenio speaks only of his grandfather. All that Arsenio would say was that his father was a great seeker of the truth and that one day he would tell Lope the story of his father's life as it was told to him by his grandparents. I think he did not want to talk of sad things to Lope during our journey north and the story of Arsenio's parents is very sad a story Arsenio has never discussed with me. But of course I learned of what happened from his grandmother.

"You see Arsenio's father was a very smart man, like Arsenio, because he too learned many things from his father Arsenio's grandfather. And one thing he learned was to love the truth and so he decided to become a journalist. And when Arsenio was still a baby his father and mother María moved to Nuevo Laredo because there was a great need for journalists in that city. Arsenio's father went to work right away for a newspaper called *El Mañana* and began to write articles about the drug cartels that were causing so much violence in the city. Three weeks later he was shot dead in front of his home. Arsenio's grandfather went to Nuevo Laredo to claim the body of his son so that it could be buried in the churchyard of the village but María did not return to the village because she no longer wanted to live in Mexico. Instead she moved to Ciudad Juárez. A cousin in El Paso said that María was working in Juárez and planned to move to Albuquerque as soon as she earned enough money to pay a coyote to take her and her baby across the border. But then she disappeared. No one knows any more than this about what happened to Arsenio's mother. So Arsenio's grandfather made another journey to claim a son, this time his grandson, Arsenio."

I hear myself say, "Jesus Christ!" I look over at Arsenio who smiles his sinister smile but I think…. Actually I don't think anything. I just feel sorry for this man I hate.

"You look depressed, Señor Thomas."

"Fuck yes I'm depressed, Imelda. What do you expect?"

"Maybe we should forget about Arsenio's parents and I will finish what Arsenio told Lope about Homer so that you will not be depressed and use such language."

"Whatever, Imelda. Yes, that's a good idea though it won't cure my depression. Only saying good-bye to your family will do that." I turn back to Imelda as I say this. I am feeling a little like those poor peasants who Arsenio says seek the blessings of the Virgin to escape their despair. Watching Imelda I think all I know about her is that she's no virgin and her presence in my home has not been a blessing. Beyond that she a mystery.

"It is unkind of you to say such a thing, Señor Thomas."

"It is not, Imelda, and you know it's not."

"Perhaps, Señor Thomas. However, as I was saying, Lope asked his father about what he was going to say about Homer because Arsenio had lost his way among all the things he desired to teach his son. And after he told Lope about the meaning of the names Lope reminded him again that he had something more to say about Homer's hero Odysseus."

"'I almost forgot, Lope, but you did not. See, you are very smart and will be a much better *soldado* than your father. But let me tell you the story of Odysseus because it explains what I have been trying to say about the gringos and why we will win against them. After the Trojan War the great Greek warrior king Odysseus spends many difficult years returning to his home where his wife and son are waiting for him. On that long journey he and his crew suffer many dangers one of which is a terrible storm that drives their ship to the island of the lotus-eaters. On this island grows the sweet leaves of the lotus plant that make a person forget all his troubles. So Odysseus' tired and weary crew eat the sweet leaves of the lotus plant and forget all about returning home. All they desire is to relax, eat the lotus leaves and enjoy the pleasant dreams they bring.

"'You see, Lope, the gringos have become like Odysseus' crew. They are weary and desire to pass their time dreaming Hollywood dreams and Super Bowl dreams and Disneyland dreams and American Idol dreams and all the other dreams that are sold to them by their dream makers who have been called puppet masters who manipulate the gringo *marionetas*. And just in case that is not sufficient *los soldados* of the Mexican drug cartels import marijuana, heroin, cocaine and many other kinds of lotus so that the gringos can dream their dreams while *los soldados de Movimiento* carry on the struggle to reclaim our Aztlán, because we Mexicans have not forgotten our homeland. We have not forgotten who we are. Thus our journey lies clearly before us while the gringos stumble into the future like a blind bull upon a rocky hilltop.'

"Then Lope asked what if the gringos awaken from their dreams.

"'They will awaken' said Arsenio, 'to find that their American dreams have become a nightmare but it will be their own fault…you know, for sleeping on the job, so to speak. What happens when you sleep on the job, Lope?'

"'You lose your job' answered Lope.

"'Exactly.'

"'But Papa, are not the gringos still the boss? And if the boss awakes and sees his workers taking over his company will he not become very angry and perhaps fire the workers? Perhaps this is what the American government will do. Perhaps they will build a big wall like that in China to keep out the Mexicans. And then what, Papa?'

"'It is good that you think of such things because to win the war against the gringo we must be very smart and tenacious and we shall be. But do not worry, Lope. Had the gringo done what you say fifty years ago he might have saved *gringolándia* but he waited too long, until it is too late. You see, my son, there are now too many of us and besides we have learned a valuable strategy from our Catholic and Hispanic brothers and sisters the Filipinos. They have a saying about their children…' And then, Señor Thomas, Arsenio was quiet for a moment because he wanted Lope to think carefully about what he was about to say.

"'And what do they say, Papa, the Filipinos?'

"'They say that America's future is the future of their children.'

"'I do not understand, Papa.'

"'It is a little mysterious but I think it means that the future of America belongs to the immigrants and each group thinks it belongs to their own people. But we know better at least for that part called *Aztlán*. It belongs to the Mexican people.'

"'And what of the American children, Papa?'

"'They will have to make do as best they can but that is none of our concern.'

"'And so is that the strategy our people learned from the Filipinos?'

"'No that is not it. It is just what they say about the future of their children being America's future. But I am glad to see that you pay attention to what your *padre* tells you. Believe me it makes him very happy.'

"And it was true, Señor Thomas. I could see it in Arsenio's eyes which looked very seriously at Lope. It was a deep affection but more than that. Arsenio understands things in a much larger way than you gringos do. I think it has to do with tradition which you gringos no longer have."

"I agree, Imelda," I say exasperatingly, feeling tired, frustrated and depressed. "We are a lost people but I knew that before you arrived to disrupt my life so please get on with your story."

"Of course, Señor Thomas. The story has almost ended." The look on Imelda's face when she spoke those words was disquieting. It seems as if there have been two Imeldas all along and just now I glimpsed the other Imelda, a fertility goddess yes but one that demanded human sacrifice. It was like seeing the dark side of the moon for the first time and realizing that behind the enchanting sheen she is but a cold hard stone.

"You are not paying attention, Señor Thomas."

"Yes I am, Imelda. Arsenio told Lope he was very happy that his son was paying attention to what his father was telling him about the strategy of the Filipinos. Right?"

"Yes that is right, Señor Thomas, and Lope responded kindly to his father because he had come to love and respect him. 'Of course, Papa,' he said, 'I will always pay attention to what you have to say. You have already taught me more than I ever knew before, so many interesting and wonderful things.'

"'And I will teach you many more once we arrive in America. But let me tell you about the strategy of the Filipinos before I forget a second time. It is called *chain migration* and again had the gringos read Homer they would know this strategy which is that *a few shall be followed by many*. Homer tells of this strategy in his poem about the war between the Greeks and the Trojans who lived in a great fortified city. After many years of trying to capture the city by force, the wily Odysseus of whom I have already spoken said the city could be captured only by treachery and suggested that the Greeks build a gigantic wooden horse and leave it outside the great wall of the city. But inside the horse were the bravest Greek soldiers just as the Mexicans who enter America illegally are the bravest Mexicans. Well of course the foolish Trojans pulled the giant wooden horse into their city even breaking a hole in the wall to do so because they thought the horse was a good thing. But then during the night while they were throwing a big party for themselves like the gringos do every night drinking their beer, eating their pizza, and watching television, wily Odysseus and his men left the horse and opened the gates allowing their compatriots waiting outside to pour into the city. And after that night the city of Troy was no more.'

"'That is a terrifying story, Papa. I feel sorry for the poor Trojans.'

"'Do not feel sorry for them, Lope, but learn from their mistake.'

"'Not to trust gifts from one's enemy, Papa?'

"'Oh my son you are very clever and one day will be as wise as Odysseus. Yes that is one of the lessons of Homer's great poem. But perhaps a bigger lesson is that disaster befalls unwise acts. Long before the Trojans foolishly brought the horse that would destroy them into their city the foolish and decadent son of the king of Troy allowed his lust to conquer his reason.'

"'And what did he do, Papa?'

"'He stole the beautiful wife of a powerful Greek king and that theft began the war between the Greeks and the Trojans.'

"'She must have been very beautiful.'

"'She was, perhaps the most beautiful woman in the world. But beauty can sometimes be a fata morgana, *un espejismo*, that can lead a man even an entire nation astray.'

"For a moment Lope was quiet. I could see that he was thinking about what his father had just told him. And then he said, 'And the gringos are like this man who stole another man's wife, Papa?'

"'Yes because they are decadent and unwise. And the price they will pay will be the loss of their nation just as the Trojans lost theirs.

"'It seems that people are very stupid, Papa.'

"'They can be and I have spoken to you about how it is very important that our people not become decadent and stupid like the gringos because when a people act unwisely they suffer greatly or even disappear.'

"'Like the Trojans?'

"'Like them and many others. Even the Greeks are no more. Those living today are no more like their great ancestors than Paris is like the great Trojan hero Hector but that is another story.'

"'And this *chain migration* that you speak of is that also found in Homer's stories?'

"'That is correct, Lope. Again you show that you are a good son because you pay attention to what your father says.'

"'But of course, Papa, but I also like the stories you tell me especially the ones by Homer because they are very strange.'

"'Yes they are very strange but very true in their own way...'

"Goddamn it, Imelda! How many of Arsenio's stories am I going to have to listen to? I'm not fucking Lope. And I really don't give a shit about what he told his son."

"You use very bad language, Señor Thomas, taking the Lord's name in vain and those other nasty words. I see you are no longer depressed but angry." She then begins gently massaging my crotch and making a humming sound.

"'Don't do that, Imelda."

"'And if I stop, you will listen to me, Señor Thomas?"

"Yes, Imelda, I will listen." As I say this I have the desire to lie down on the floor and rest. But I know I shouldn't and a quick glance at the rest of her family watching us with amused expressions confirms that I must not lie down. "Go on, Imelda. Go on with your stories" I say feeling as if I'm in a dream world.

"Thank you, Señor Thomas, I will but remember I tell these stories for you not for myself."

"Yes, Imelda, I know, I know. Please continue."

"So Arsenio said to Lope, 'Do you remember, Lope, what strategy the Greeks were using when they left the great wooden horse?'

"'Yes, Papa, that *a few shall be followed by many.*'

"'Excellent, Lope. Well the Filipino immigrants who come to America use a similar strategy which I have told you is called *chain migration.* And the way it works is this: for every Filipino who arrives in America ten family members will follow but I shall give you an example of my own that will show you how we Mexicans also use this strategy. Imagine a rivulet that divides two ant territories, one very crowded, the other very spacious and not crowded at all. In the crowded territory millions of ants wait desperately to cross the rivulet.'

"'Like the Mexicans who wait to cross the Rio Grande.'

"'Yes, exactly, but there are many other immigrants like the Filipinos who seek to cross other rivulets that are not so small like the Pacific Ocean. On one side of the rivulet are millions of ants their numbers increasing every day even every hour. They are very crowded and there is not sufficient food for them because their numbers are so great. And on the other side of the rivulet there is much empty land and not so many ants except in the cities, *los hormigueros*. The ants that live in that spacious territory are very fat and lazy and spend their time lying on their backs sunning themselves, living off the abundance of the land and the bounty created for them by their great ancestors, a race of ants that are no more.'

"Lope, laughed at this and said 'The fat lazy ants are gringo ants yes, Papa?'

"'Exactly. So what do the smart hungry ants do? I will tell you. The males among them, because the males are the ones who are responsible for the family in such a situation, take twigs to the rivulet and make small bridges to cross over. But because they are a very clever, they know that the bridges will be used many times by their relatives who will follow in the days, months and years to come.'

"'But, Papa, I understand how the bridges work for ants but the gringos would not allow such bridges. They would destroy them, no?'

"'Yes they would. The bridges I speak of are legal bridges. You see American laws make each immigrant into a small bridge for his entire family. Do you see now how the chain works? The first family member crosses the bridge but all the members of the family are holding hands each helping the others to cross.'

"'Yes, Papa, I see. It is a very beautiful story. But I do not understand why the gringos would allow such a thing. I mean in Mexico almost everyone is related.'

"'Who knows, Lope? What you say is true but as I have said many times the gringos are an ignorant people. Perhaps it is because in a way that is *muy malo* the gringos are truly the *mañana* people living only for today and caring nothing for tomorrow. It is well known that the gringos do not love the earth as we do. They pollute the water, air and sky; they destroy their ancient forests; and now their SUVs are changing the climate of the world. And if you say to them *Hey, gringo, look at what you are doing to the earth! You are ruining it for your grandchildren*, they will say only *Let mañana take care of itself. Today we are fat and happy, and that is all that matters.*

"'But what do we care, Lope? Their stupidity is our good fortune because all along the rivulet that separates Mexico from America are millions of twigs each carrying a constant stream of Latino *hormigas* into a new territory which once belonged to them and will again one day because now as always there exists two Mexicos, one south of the border, the other north of the border. And in truth there is no real border. It is a figment of the gringo's imagination. Ha ha ha…'

"Señor Thomas, Lope and I could not help but smile at Arsenio's laughter because it was a happy laughter. But then he grew serious again and continued to speak of why you gringos will not be able to stop us.

"'But the little bridges are not the only reason the gringo cannot stop us, Lope. The gringo has become like fat lazy ants that spend their time in the sun but he is much worse. You see, the immigrants are his drug and like the drug addict who cannot do without his crack or meth or heroin, he hates his addiction but cannot live without it. So just as the gringo cannot do without the drugs that come from south of the border and all over the world, he cannot do without the Latino immigrants he has come to depend on. We are the drug the gringo cannot live without. And that is why we will be victorious. And if the gringo politicians decide to get tough on immigration because their ratings in the polls are low it will mean only a battle lost in the war to regain *Aztlán*. Victory will be postponed a little longer but only a little. Beside, Lope, *El Movimiento* is our life and regaining *Aztlán* is our destiny. It is a holy war that we fight, like that of the insurgents in Iraq. The gringo government has many soldiers in Iraq but everyone knows they will not win because the hearts of the gringo people are not in the war but our hearts beat only for one thing, the return of our people to *Aztlán*.'

"Lope could see that his father was very serious about the struggle of the Mexican people to regain their ancient homeland *Aztlán* and told Arsenio that he understood the importance of *El Movimiento*. But then he said, 'I understand, Papa, that the gringos would not be interested in fighting for Iraq a place which is not their homeland nor a threat to it but I do not understand that they would not fight for America, which is their homeland.'

"'Yes it seems strange, Lope, but I will tell you why the gringo does not defend his homeland. It is because he has forgotten his homeland. He has no nostalgia because his heart is filled with the hoopla, *la barahunda*, of the present moment. The gringo has forgotten who he was. He lives without memory. He exists in a state of amnesia.'

"'But why, Papa? How can such a thing be forgotten?'

"'Lope, do you remember the story about the carnival and the carnies who leave the village to go away with the carnival?'

"'Yes of course.'

"'Well you see if you stay away long enough you forget the village and its people and you no longer know who you are. For such a person there is nothing to defend, nothing to fight for.'

"'I understand now, Papa. The gringos live in forgetfulness.'

"'Very good, Lope. I see that my son is becoming wise.'

"It was clear that Lope's understanding of such things greatly pleased Arsenio. But one evening Lope said to Arsenio that he would like to know how we would cross the border?

"'Lope, do you think your father has not thought about such things? That I would bring my family to America without a plan?'

"'No, Papa, of course not. It's just that this is all new for me. And there has been talk about the crossing becoming more difficult because there are many more police patrolling the border and sometimes I wonder what will happen to the family if we are caught by the gringo border police. What will happen to us then, Papa?'

"Then Arsenio realized that Lope was not afraid for himself but for his family and I think, Señor Thomas, Arsenio also remembered what it was like for him when he first sneaked into America. Arsenio's face changed and I could see he was proud that Lope was concerned for his family.

"'You are right, Lope. I had forgotten that I too was a little afraid the first time I entered America. It is a powerful country but less powerful than it looks on TV and we have many many friends on both sides of the border. For example, do not be afraid of the border patrol. They are no match for the charms of your mother. Do you remember the wise poet Homer of whom I spoke?'

"'Of course, the stories about the lotus-eaters and the great wooden horse. How could I forget such stories?'

"'Well, Lope, Homer also speaks of a goddess by the name of Circe who was able to cast a spell upon men and she did so to Odysseus's crew turning them into *puercos* who were then under her power.'

"'Into pigs! That is very strange, Papa. She must have had great magic.'

"'It is not as strange as you would think, Lope. All women have a little bit of Circe's magic.'

"'And you think Mamma has such magic?'

"'Oh yes. Your mother has *mucha magia*.'

"Is it true, Señor Thomas, that I have such magic?"

"Yes, Imelda it is true. You're a sorceress and have succeeded in turning yours truly into a pig no doubt about that. Please get on with your story."

"Yes, of course, Señor Thomas, but you must admit that you were a happy pig."

"Perhaps for a while I was a happy pig but not now."

"I am sorry for your unhappiness, Señor Thomas, and now I will finish Arsenio's story. He explained to Lope that I would cast the spell of love upon any border guard who might stop us in the night."

"'You see, Lope,' he said, 'not only does your mother have great charms but most of the men of the border patrol are Latinos, who of course prefer to make love rather than to make war against their own people.'

"'But, Papa, why do not the gringos guard their border?'

"'Because, as you know, gringos speak only English and so they must rely on our people to protect them.'

"'But that's like the fox guarding the hen-house.'

"'Yes, Lope, something like that because the Mexican people are foxes who want to get into the gringo hen-house and many of the border guards are also foxes as well, foxes who, as I said, do not wish to make war against their own kind especially if given the opportunity to make love to a beautiful Latina *zorra*.'

"'And the gringos, Papa, who are they in this story?'

"'They are the farmer who hates the foxes who come upon his property and eats his chickens. Would it not be better for the farmer if he used dogs instead of foxes to guard his property from foxes?'

"'Yes of course, Papa.'

"'Ha ha ha ha ha ha.'

"Arsenio laughed very much and finally Lope asked, 'Why do you laugh so much, Papa?'

"'Our stories about ants and pigs and hens and foxes and dogs—they are very funny don't you agree, Lope?'

"'Yes, but I hope that when we cross the border the border patrol will be Latino foxes and not gringo dogs.'

"'Do not worry, Lope. We will encounter neither foxes nor dogs for we shall go beneath the border.'

"'We shall dig our way, Papa?'

"'No, my son, we shall do no digging. That has been done already. We shall pay some money to the men who have dug the tunnel and then walk beneath the border, invisible to border patrol. And, Lope, I will tell you one more thing that will put your mind at ease. If we cannot use the tunnels because too many illegal immigrants are using them that night then we will simply have a gringo drive us across the border.'

"'Papa, you are kidding, no?'

"'No. I know it seems impossible but gringos drive illegal immigrants across the border every day. These drivers are known as *monos*, monkeys, because the monkey has no dignity and will do anything for a banana. You see, Lope, *Gringolándia* has become a land of monkeys and money has become the gringo's banana. But I have already spoken of these things. So do not worry about your family, Lope. There are many tunnels both above and below the ground like the little bridges of the ants that will take us safely into the U.S. So if one is closed we shall use another. Do not worry, my son.'

"'Thank you, Papa. I do not worry now. I see you are very wise and will take care of us.'

"'And you are a good son the best any father could ask for. And we shall work together like a family, each one of us doing his and her part. And remember that we belong to a much bigger family the Latino family. We are not alone like the gringos who live alone and fight among themselves. When you are in the barrio you are among family and if you listen very hard you will hear whispered among our brothers and sisters, *Sí, se hará. Sí, se hará.*'

"'I wish we were there now, Papa.'

"'It will not be much longer, Lope, and the first thing we shall do when we get to America is vacate a home in San Diego.'

"'I do not understand, Papa,' said Lope."

"Yeah, Imelda, I don't fucking understand either."

"There is no need for such language, Señor Thomas."

"Fuck there isn't. What is this vacating all about?"

"Señor Thomas, I was just about to let Arsenio explain but you interrupted me."

"Get on with it, damn it!"

"Señor Thomas, you seem a little irritated. Is Imelda teasing you? Because if she is I will tell her to stop. Hee, hee, hee."

I look up and see Arsenio snickering. The rest of the family now sit quietly as if waiting for something to happen. I just stare at the man realizing for the first time in what now seems like years that perhaps their invasion of my home had been orchestrated. Arsenio and I had been playing a game of chess but I am just now finding that out. The fucking fox. My anger dissolves into simmering resentment. I turn back to Imelda.

"So, Imelda, tell me what Arsenio told Lope about vacating a home in San Diego." As I say this I look closely at her mocha brown face and see that it's very beautiful in an earthly, exotic way, like Gauguin's paintings of the Tahitian women but more mysterious like the exotic paintings of Rousseau. Her eyes are so dark that I cannot distinguish the pupils from the irises. Her teeth are white like polished ivory and her lips are full. Her skin is smooth and radiates health. Hers is not the beauty you see in a Hollywood movie or on a fashion runway. It is old, ancient, as if it grew directly from the earth. And her expression is so peaceful and reassuring. I feel really fucked. Imelda is a beautiful erotic mystery that has entangled me just as the black widow's suitor becomes entangled in her web.

"Señor Thomas! Are you listening?"

"Yes, Imelda, I'm listening. What was it you said?"

"I said that Arsenio told Lope that we shall rid the house of its gringo occupants."

"'But are we not going to live in L.A., Papa?' responded Lope.

"'Of course Lope,' said his father. "For now we are going to live in the Latino city of Maywood which is next door to L.A. and very much a Mexican city because ninety-seven percent of the people are Latino and only two percent are gringo but you will never see them because they stay in their houses. But I'm thinking we will soon need a bigger house because as you see our family has grown much larger. But the house in Maywood is a very nice house a mansion compared to our house in our village. It once belonged to a gringo family who like all the other gringos left the city as the homes were vacated. I am very certain that you will love Maywood, Lope, because it will be as if you never left Mexico but you will have all the benefits of living in America.

"'Also, this city is also a very special city because it is a *sanctuary city* for illegal immigrants and all of us are illegal. Like us, the city council and the mayor hate the gringo and are following the lead of the gringo cardinal His Holiness Roger Mahony by making the city a sanctuary for our people. And soon there shall be hundreds of Sanctuary Cities declared by duly elected mayors and city councils. Again this is an example of how we shall use democracy to defeat the gringos at their own game. And I shall tell you a secret, Lope, but first can you tell me what a secret is?'

"'I believe it is a meaning that is kept hidden, Papa.'

"'That is right, my son, and in America there are many meanings that are hidden from the gringo, and the one I speak of now is most important and it is amazing that the gringos have not discovered it.' And Lope became very excited and leaned closer to his father to better hear this great secret.

"'Yes, Papa?'

"'It is this: When a city is declared a Sanctuary City it becomes a Mexican city a part of Mexico.'

"'And the gringos do not know this?'

"'No they do not.'

"'That is truly amazing, Papa. So why must we vacate a house in San Diego if we have a nice home in the American Mexican city of Maywood?'

"'We must think of the future. San Diego is a beautiful city and not so polluted and crime ridden and congested as L.A. So we shall vacate a home in San Diego and allow it to be used as a safe house for a few years for the others who follow us. We do this for our people just as those who came before us vacated thousands of gringo homes and cities for us. And we shall make a little money besides. Unlike the gringo, Lope, we shall work together to first reclaim *Aztlán* and then to occupy the rest of America like New York and Chicago which are not part of *Aztlán* but are a part of the growing Hispanic Nation of America. Already the gringo children in those cities are a tiny minority as the Latino children multiply by the thousands.'

"And now you know, Señor Thomas, all that Arsenio told his son during our journey here."

"So it's our house that is being vacated as you call it?"

"Of course, you silly man," she says, looking at me with that bewitching look of hers.

"I will not allow that to happen, Imelda."

"I know, Señor Thomas. You are a good man." Saying this she smiles provocatively and as she does so I again become aware of her beautiful breasts still hanging outside her blouse. I cannot resist staring at them. It's as if they're the North Pole and my eyes are two compasses.

"You like my watermelons don't you, Señor Thomas? Touch them."

"No, I won't touch them."

"Yes one last time."

"No I won't touch them. You should cover yourself, Imelda. I'm very tired."

"I know, Señor Thomas."

"'I'm going into the kitchen."

"But I have not told you what happened to my second husband and you said you wanted to know."

"Oh, Imelda!' I say wearily. Her presence is like a narcotic that puts one into a hypnotic stupor."

"Then you do not want to know?"

"Yes I want to know but please make it quick."

"If that is your wish, Señor Thomas. As I said before, when Arsenio returned he and Lope went off together. And after talking a long time and drinking many beers they returned."

Then, bringing her face close to mine as if she was telling me a secret, Imelda says, "Arsenio and Lope came back home and announced to me and Amancio that they were going to America and they asked me if I would go with them and take the children. And of course I said I would.

"Well as you would expect, Amancio was furious. He called me a whore and said I could go with them but the children would stay with him. I told Arsenio that I would not leave my children. So Arsenio invited Amancio to go with us saying that America was very big and had plenty of room for all of us. Amancio said to Arsenio that he only wanted to fuck his wife, and Arsenio said that I was his wife too and that they both could fuck me. In that way Arsenio is very generous. But Amancio said he didn't want to fuck me anymore and told Arsenio that he should leave.

"By this time the two men were yelling and calling one another the most awful names. I was crying hysterically and the children were crying too. And I did not know what to do. I wanted to go to America and thought Amancio very unreasonable to prevent me and his children from going to America and to expect us to stay in our village which has been all my life a place of despair.

When I first met Arsenio long before we married he talked about going to America and taking me with him. And that was my dream and the only reason I married him. Look at him. He is an ugly man not as nearly as handsome as Amancio who looked very much like Ricky Martin but I wanted to go to America yet a woman cannot go alone. She would be killed and buried like the women of Juárez. And once in America it would not matter if I was married to Arsenio because I would be in America."

"Imelda," I interrupted, "does this story have an ending?"

"Oh yes, Señor Thomas, a terrible ending."

"Well what is it?"

"I will tell you. While Arsenio and Amancio argued, Lope went into the kitchen and got the big knife I used for cutting meat, returned to where the two men were arguing, and stabbed Amancio in the back. Then he pulled it out and stabbed him again. By then Arsenio had taken out his knife and started stabbing Amancio in the chest. Amancio fell to the floor and Arsenio and Lope kept stabbing him Arsenio calling him *un traidor*. There was blood everywhere. The children became very quiet and Arsenio told me to take them to the bedroom and pack for the trip. Then he and Lope wrapped Amancio in the rug he was lying on. Lope borrowed a truck and they took Amancio away from the village and buried him. Then we started our journey to America."

"Jesus, Imelda. So both Arsenio and Lope are murderers. And you let them into my home. Goddamn you!"

"Yes, Señor Thomas, that is true but as I said we had some trouble with the car so we had no choice but to come here."

"Well weren't we the lucky ones!" I look around the room at the graffiti-covered walls. As the *loco* family sits quietly watching me I look at the two goons Arsenio and Lope. I suppose they are wondering what I am going to do. For myself I'm more in a state of dumbfoundedness than preparation.

"You should have told me, Imelda. I didn't think you were as bad as your son and husband. I thought of you as being their prisoner or something as it seems we are."

"I guess you don't love Imelda anymore." I look at her curiously. Her breasts are still exposed. *Jesus, she's riddle, a fucking sphinx, and I totally misread her and am now paying the price.*

"You like my watermelons don't you, Señor Thomas? Touch them."

"No, I won't touch them."

"Yes, one last time and I will not bother you any longer since you no longer like me."

Believing what she says, I touch them.

"There are you satisfied?"

"You see, you foolish donkey, why we shall win? I too am *un soldado* and I have conquered you with my two *bombas*. You cannot fight a woman so how are you going to fight a man?" I jerk my hands away.

"Fuck you, Imelda," realizing that I hate the woman but also that she is right just as Anne was right.

"Please fuck me, Señor Thomas. Put your dick inside me and let me give you pleasure," and then she suddenly grabs my pants. I pull her hand away shaking my head in disbelief at the power she has had over me. *God damn her!* But say nothing more to her. Words are as much a web as her titties so I turn and walk silently into the kitchen but as I do I can hear in the background guffawing like the braying of a donkey. *That fucking Arsenio!*

Anne and Kelly are sitting at the table. Anne looks as if she had just emerged from a grave. Kelly is pale and distraught. Her face is bruised. Two phones lie on the table.

"What happened to your face?" I ask.

"I hurt it in the car."

"In the car? What were you doing there?"

"I was sleeping."

"Why in the car?"

"Didn't you notice," Anne interrupts, "that her room has been occupied?"

"I'm sorry, honey. I didn't realize..."

"No, you haven't realized a lot of things, Jeffrey," Anne says.

"I'm sorry. I really am but I'm going to deal with the problem right now. What about 911? Any luck there?"

"Yeah, lots of luck. Didn't you hear the police sirens outside?"

"I don't think the sarcasm is helpful right now, Anne. I assume you've gotten no response from the police."

"That's right Jeffrey but why should we expect the police to pay attention to us when we can't even get you to pay attention?"

"Mom, please stop."

When Kelly speaks I begin to realize how distraught she is. "I'm sorry, Kelly" I tell her. "I've been occupied with the family."

"Oh we know you've been busy," says Anne. "I've seen and am quite impressed by the attention you've paid to them. But I guess it's now your family's turn to receive some of your attention."

"Yes," I say and sit down at the table. "Kelly, I didn't realize how hard all this has been on you but I promise you it's almost over." Anne looks at me incredulously and Kelly just stares blankly.

"It's true Kelly" I continue. "It will soon be over."

"Kelly, tell your father what you just told me" Anne interrupts. "I know it's hard but he needs to know."

"What is it? Is there something I don't know?"

"You are such an idiot, Jeffrey," Anne interjects.

I feel myself becoming frightened. *Something awful has happened.* I turn to Kelly. "What happened, Kelly? Please tell me." But she still doesn't speak only keeps looking down at the table her eyes red apparently from hours of crying.

"Anne, do you know what happened?"

"Three men did something to her..." she says, her voice trailing off, her gaze turning downward toward her hands, each embracing the other as if they were trying to consoling one another.

"Oh God! What? What? Tell me," I say, raising my voice. "Those fuckers out there?" I stand up to go out to the living room. Then Kelly speaks.

"Dad, don't leave us again. Please don't leave us."

"I won't. I promise I won't." Then I think about what Imelda told me about Arsenio and Lope killing her second husband.

Looking up and directly into my eyes, Anne says, "We must leave."

"We can't just leave. This is our home," I tell her.

"Not now, not anymore," she says resolutely.

"I don't understand. I'll just get rid of those people. I think we have come to an understanding."

"An understanding? Oh Jeffrey, as they would say, you are such an *estúpido*. Don't you see what's going on? Haven't you noticed that you have been trying to get rid of them for days and have gotten nowhere? Besides I don't want you to."

"Why not?"

"It's too dangerous. They are dangerous people. They are not like us. They're like desperate animals."

"Dad," Kelly says in a pleading voice. "Do you have a gun?"

"No I don't. Why, honey?"

"I'm afraid."

"Don't be, honey. Dad's going to take care of this right now."

"No don't. They will kill you. The men said they would kill you."

"Who said that? Arsenio and Lope?"

"The young one and his friends."

"Friends? There are others?"

"Yes two others with tattoos."

"When did this happen? Where? I don't understand. What happened?"

"In the garage. When I saw the graffiti I went to the garage and hid in the car but they must have seen me."

"Who?"

"The man in the living room and two others. I was asleep in the car when they came. One of them opened the door and put his hand over my mouth. He told me not to scream. He had a gun and said that if I screamed you and mom would come and he would kill you both. I begged them to go away but they wouldn't. He then told me to get out of the car and when I was out he told me to take off my clothes. I didn't want to. I was too scared. So he started tearing at them, ripping them off. I started crying and he told me to shut up but I couldn't help it, so he hit me. I kept on crying so one of the other men said 'Shut up bitch' and hit me hard in the face."

"Oh, fucking God, I'll kill them."

"No, no, Dad. They will *kill* you. I don't want to be alone. Please don't do anything."

Suddenly I feel a great weariness settling upon me. "Go on, honey. Tell me what happened."

"They pushed me back into the car and then they took turns. I wanted to scream but I was afraid they would hurt you and Mom. When they were done one of them said that if I wanted my parents alive I'd better keep to myself what happened. He said they would be back for more. I tried not to say anything but I am so afraid and have nowhere to hide."

"It's better that you told us. We'll do something."

"Do what?" asked Anne. "Call the police?"

I look at Kelly thinking *I have failed*. It's too late to undo what has happened to her. She experienced terror in her own home and I failed to protect her.

"I must talk to those people. I am going to tell them they must leave."

"Oh Dad, don't."

"Don't worry, Kelly, I won't do anything stupid." Now I wish I had a gun so I could exterminate the whole lot of them. Anne was right. I've been blind. Fucking blind.

"Let me speak to them. If I can't get them to leave then we will leave. Okay?"

"Okay, Dad."

I return to the living room unsure of how much I should say to them or of what I am going to do. There they are a family from hell.

"Señor Thomas," Arsenio greets me, "It's good to have you back. How is the family?"

"I think you know."

"You mean the little one? How can you resent the boys' having a little fun after amusing yourself?"

"You sleaze bag..."

"I am sorry for what happened. I did not know but as you know boys will be boys. Besides, your little girl is now a woman too and for that she should be grateful."

"You need to get the hell out of the house. I've called the police and if you leave now you and your sick family might be able to disappear back into the swamp you came out of."

"I detect *mucho* hostility in the tone of you voice, Señor Thomas, which is completely uncalled for and could be detrimental to your health. And as far as the police are concerned you are wasting your time. They are very busy today."

As he spoke Lope pulled out a very big knife and opened it. Imelda shakes her head as to say *I told you so*. Now I understand why those right-wing gun nuts own guns. This kind of shit probably only happens to pacifist Green Party members like me. At this moment I would give anything for an assault rifle.

"You're not leaving then is that it?"

"Señor Thomas, we just got here. That is the problem with you gringo Americans. You have no hospitality, no *Mi casa es tu casa*, which is very uncivilized."

"I think you mean to say *Tu casa es mi casa*. Isn't that right?"

"No we are only your guests and will leave as soon as my cousin Santhrax fixes the car and brings it to us."

"And I suppose you don't know when that will be and that you cannot call him."

"That is true. He is not a wealthy man and has no phone so we must be patient."

Lope is still playing with his knife and Imelda is smiling at me but it is not the sweet smile of before. The two children of the dead father now look more like the children of the corn than ordinary children. I am certain they will follow in the footsteps of their mother and stepfather. A tempest of human dysfunctionality has swept into our home and I have been too simpleminded to see what was happening. I realize that the situation has evolved beyond my control. The only solution now is to run away just as they, I suppose, ran away from the nightmare south of the border. In doing so however they brought that nightmare into my home. *These people are monsters but monsters are made, not born.*

"You win," I tell Arsenio and walk back toward the kitchen.

"You also, Señor Thomas. We are all winners."

HaHahaHahaHaHaHahaHahaHa
HaHahaHahaHaHahaHa
HaHahaHahaHa
HahaHaha
HahaHa
Haha
HA!"

A whirlwind of demonic laughter fills the room, perfectly complementing the visual nightmare of the graffiti-covered walls. They had succeeded in creating an atmosphere that is unbearable. The only choice left to us is to flee.

In the kitchen Anne and Kelly are still sitting at the table their faces filled with despair.

"Well, Dad, are they leaving?"

"They're certainly not leaving, right Jeffrey?" Anne says, acid dripping off each word.

But I ignore her caustic tone and announce to Kelly with as much optimism as I can muster, which isn't very much, "Your mother's right. You both should pack a suitcase as quickly as possible and we will go to a hotel and contact the police." I then walk over to one of the kitchen drawers and take out a medium-sized butcher knife."

"What are you going to do with that, Jeffrey?" Anne asks.

"Nothing I hope. But if they interfere I'm going to shove it into one of them, which one, man, woman, or child, doesn't matter. They all seem equally Satan's spawn. Stick together and get packed. If any of them come near you scream and I will come. I'm going to the garage to get the car ready and maybe find a more effective weapon. God I wish I had a gun. Go on now."

Anne and Kelly leave the kitchen and I go to the laundry room, which opens into the garage. I turn on the light and see that the windshield has been smashed and the tires slashed. On two walls of the garage book shelves with doors have been opened and the books removed and thrown onto the floor. I climb over the books in front of the car to get to the driver side, though I'm not sure why, only to discover books piled a foot or more on that side of the car. Suddenly the thought of what happened in the car sickens me and I realize that Kelly would be too terrified to get into the car.

I give up on the car and look for another weapon. I'm thinking there is a good chance that I'll cut myself with the knife stuck into the back of my pants. Among the gardening tools there should be a hatchet but it's missing. Panic begins to take hold of me as I imagine Lope chopping up Anne and Kelly. I quickly leave the garage and hurry through the laundry room to the kitchen where I find Anne and Kelly looking like frightened refugees waiting to escape an approaching holocaust.

"Thank God," I say letting out a sigh of relief. "Did they bother you?"

"No," says Anne, "they're still in the living room. Waiting for us to leave I guess. I have never encountered creepier people in my entire life. They've turned our lives into a horror show."

"Well let's get the hell out of this house of horrors," I say and touch the handle of the knife. I decided that if any one of them approaches us I would just start stabbing like Jason in *Friday the 13th*.

"Hey you guys, if they try to keep us from leaving I want you to drop the suitcases and run."

"What about you, Dad? I don't want anything to happen to you."

"The best thing you can do for me is escape and go to the Blairs for help. Okay?"

"Okay," says Kelly with a scared look that made me sad to see.

"Let's go," I say. They each pick up a suitcase and I start for the door to the living room.

"Aren't we taking the car?" Anne asks.

"No, they sabotaged it."

"Oh God!" she groans.

"It will be fine," I say with mocked confidence. We leave the kitchen and find the family still sitting in the living room. The backdrop of sprayed graffiti makes the nightmare complete. *How stupid I've been.*

"Hey, Señor Thomas, both our families are finally together. What a wonderful moment for us, yes?" says Arsenio. I do not respond. I think only of getting Anne and Kelly out of the house.

"Oh, I see. You are not happy with Arsenio," he continues.

I open the door and wait for Anne and Kelly to go outside and then follow them. Just as I go out the door Arsenio calls out, "*Chiau*, Señor Thomas. Don't be a stranger."

I look back and say, "Fuck you! Arsenio."

"That's not a very nice thing to say, Señor Thomas. It would be better for all of us if you gringos were not so intolerant. Then we could all live happily together. Ha ha ha ha..."

I can hear his laughter even after I shut the door. *Fuck, what an idiot I've been!* As much as I hate fucking Arsenio I have to admit that he has done a better job looking out for his family than I have looking out for mine.

I catch up with the girls at the sidewalk. "Let's go to the Blairs. Maybe Tim or Cheryl will be there." They are the only people we know well on our street.

"Dad, I don't want to stay here," Kelly pleads.

"We won't honey. We'll just call a cab. Or maybe one of Blairs can drive us to a police station and we can report what has happened. Then we will find a hotel away from all this."

"Okay. That sounds great, Dad," she says, her child-like voice filled with a desperate optimism. It is the same tone of voice she had when she was six or seven. Kelly's become a little girl again and I feel a deep, empty sadness within me. The horror of what has happened to her is overwhelming. She is so good and precious. I recall how she would call me if she found a spider in her room but asked me not to kill it, only to take it outside—where in all probability it was eaten by some predator. I allowed irrevocable harm to come to her. I feel an unbearable despair for being so weak. I'm sad because such evil exists in the world. I am overwhelmed by the fear that I will not be able to protect her. Then I think I must stop thinking about such things or else we shall never escape. I must remain strong for Kelly and Anne, who both now depend upon me.

We come to the Blairs' house. "Wait here," I say and go up the steps. I knock on the door. I want to look back at Anne and Kelly but I'm afraid of what I might see in their faces.

The door opens and a Mexican woman who looks like an older Imelda stands before me."

"What do you want?" she asks in a heavy Mexican accent and menacing tone. Perhaps she's a cleaning woman having a very bad day but who am I kidding? Like Anne, Cheryl isn't the kind of woman to use domestic help. Once I suggested to Anne that she should have a cleaning woman come in a couple times a month. She said, "My home isn't a plantation. I'll do the work myself, though a little help from you once in a while wouldn't hurt."

"I would like to speak to Tim or Cheryl, please," I say to the woman in a friendly tone of voice. My mother always told me that it pays to be nice. How wrong she was but I thought I'd give it another try.

"They don't live here anymore," she says dully.

"That can't be. I just spoke to Tim a few days ago."

"They are gone. They don't live here now," she says in the same flat, matter-of-fact tone.

I feel myself being gripped by apprehension. *Something is very wrong.* "I don't understand," I respond.

Then the door opens wider and two Hispanic men appear. They wear bandanas on their heads and wife-beater T-shirts. Their hair is buzzed cut in the style of gang members and both wear extensive tattoos on their arms and necks. I cannot imagine human beings looking more terrifying unless it be the German SS in their Nazi uniforms. One of the men holds a chain leash attached to a barbed collar around the neck of an equally menacing-looking gray and white pit bull. The other says, "She said they don't live here anymore. Don't you understand English, *cabrón?*" The man holding the dog gives the leash a mean, hard jerk and the dog suddenly transforms into a vicious, barking, growling beast lunging toward me. I have no doubt it would tear me to pieces if its master let go of the leash.

"Oh no, no, no," I hear behind me. "No, no." It's Kelly. I turn around thinking that she's been attacked.

I hurry over to her and say, "What's wrong, baby?" nervously glancing back at the man and pit bull that's growling like an idling chain saw.

"They are the other two men."

"Hey, Señor, you can leave your daughter and wife. We will take good care of them," says one of the men, and I turn to them and shout, "*Fucking filth!*"

Then the one with the dog says, "*Lárgate!*, gringo, before I set my dog onto your daughter."

"*Hahahahahahahahaha!*" All three, even the woman, are laughing. *God I hate them!* Frightened to death that the man will let go of the dog and it will attack Kelly, I turn to find her.

"Jeffrey!" Anne yells from the sidewalk. "What are you doing for God's sake? Let's get away from these people." Kelly has taken off down the street while I was watching the three demons at the door. I run after her as fast as I can. In the distance behind me I hear one of the men yell, "Don't be a stranger, stranger." Then begins a cacophony of demonic laughter, "*Hahahahahahahahaha!*" counterpointed with Cerberus' menacing barking and growling. Thankfully the hellish noise fades as I run after Kelly.

As I'm running I wonder about the Blairs' daughter Sabrina who is only six or seven. I imagine her and her mother locked in the laundry room to be used as sex slaves, Tim stuffed in the trunk of his car. Thank God Kelly finally stops, allowing me to catch up with her. When I reach her she is on her knees with her face in her hands, sobbing uncontrollably.

I kneel down and hold her tight. Still trying to catch my breath, I say, "Let's wait for your mother, baby."

"Oh, Daddy, oh Daddy," she cries. What can you say, that *it's all going to be fine*? I am about to break into tears. Carrying the suitcases Anne finally catches up to us. *Poor Anne!* I take one of one of suitcases and start walking.

"Come on, let's get out of here."

"Mom, I can carry my suitcase." Kelly takes her suitcase from Anne and looks at me.

"I'm okay, Dad," she says and gives me a smile. I look at her bruised face. *She's a terrific kid.*

After about ten minutes Kelly says, "Dad, have you noticed the flags hanging from the houses?"

I had noticed but said nothing. Almost every house has a flag of one size or another and though they look something like American flags, they aren't.

The seven red stripes have been changed to green and where the stars had been is an emblem of a brown eagle against a red background holding a serpent in its claw and beak. It stands on a cactus and below it in the middle of a half circle floral design is a miniature tricolor Mexican flag. The flag is an amalgamation of the American and Mexican flags. I recall Victor Frankenstein's attempt to create a perfect human from the body parts of various dead people. What he got instead was a monster. *That fucking Arsenio!* I think. He played simple but he isn't. He's as crafty as a fox and I shudder to think that all his people are as crafty as he is.

"Yeah kinda weird, huh?" I say to her dumbly as if I don't understand what they mean.

"Scary weird, Dad, like the people. Haven't you noticed they're now all Mexicans? Where are all our old neighbors? What's happening, Dad?" I look back. Her blue eyes are frightened yet I can see that it's still okay as long as her dad is here. Her trust in me makes my heart sink and fills me with self-disgust. I smile the best I can.

"Yeah I noticed, babe, but I'm not sure what's going on."

I notice all right. The clumps of people talking together; children playing on the sidewalk and in the yards; a man washing his car; a woman digging in her garden; a group of young men gathered at a street corner, like the two at the Blairs' house, wearing helmet haircuts, tattoos, and mean looks, one of whom shouts as we pass by, "Hey homey! Aren't you in the wrong hood?" They're all Hispanic. It seems that except for us all the people in the neighborhood are Hispanic, Mexicans, I presume, but who knows. They stare as we walk by as if we're from another planet. Most say nothing but their looks make it clear that we are unwelcome strangers tolerated only because we are leaving. *We have become strangers in our own neighborhood, run out by the pit-bull people.* But I keep my thoughts to myself. Things are already bad enough for Kelly, for all of us.

"And the graffiti, it's everywhere. God! I am frightened, Jeffrey," says Anne in a shaky voice. I know she's worried not so much for herself or even me but for Kelly. In Anne's voice I can hear the fear of a mother feeling helpless and panicky.

"We are going to keep walking," I say, but just then occurs the most disturbing event of our escape thus far. As we pass by a yard where three children are playing, the children start picking up rocks, big rocks, and throwing them at us. We try to hurry away but one hits Anne in the face.

"Ooooh," she cries and falls to her knees. I run over to her.

"Oh God, Anne, are you okay?" I ask, blood pouring from a cut on her cheek just below her right eye. "Come on, baby, get up. We've got to keep going."

"You fucking little monsters!" *God, it's Kelly.* She's picking up the rocks and throwing them back, hitting one of them, a big girl, who starts screaming.

"Kelly!" I yell, "get away from them. Get back over here." Fortunately we have been walking in the street near the gutter in order to stay as far away as possible from the houses. Had we been closer God only knows how many rocks would have hit us.

"You fucking little monsters," Kelly screams again. "I'll come back and kill you for what you did to my mother." She's furious and sobbing at the same time. I think of my knife. I could run up to the little demons and stab each one of them but I imagine the door opening and tattooed gangsters and pit bulls pouring out of the house to destroy us. Hearing Kelly and seeing what she's doing, Anne gets up and says, "We *must* get her out of here, Jeffrey."

"I know, Anne. Come on." I hold her around the waist and hurry her toward the middle of the street.

"Kelly, get over here!" I yell. She hurries over and takes her mother's arm and we continue on our way down the street. Thankfully there is no traffic. In a weird way the neighborhood has become a ghost town and we have become human tumbleweeds.

"Dad, one day I'm going to come back and kill those people. They're not like us. Where are our people, Dad?"

"I'm not sure, Kelly. We just need to find them." I'm thinking that hell doesn't need fire and brimstone. It can be a neighborhood just like ours. We continue on as fast as we can with Anne, who is still dazed by the blow to her face. Seeing the blood splattered over her blouse and skirt, I too feel faint. It's not the blood but that it's *Anne's* blood.

"Our suitcases, where are our suitcases, Jeffrey?"

"Don't worry about them, honey, we will buy what we need when we get to a hotel." I look back to where we left the suitcases. The children have opened them and are gathered around their contents like ants around a dead beetle. Laughing madly they throw the contents into the air and about the street. As we continue on, other children throw rocks at us as we pass by. Fortunately most of the children are only five to ten years of age and select the biggest rocks they can find so that most do not reach us. The scene is surreal—

the small children, their faces filled with hatred, struggling to toss the largest rocks possible, some of which are so large that they fall only a few feet in front of the throwers. *Thank God for big stones and small hands*, I think. Lucky for us the parents and older siblings are satisfied just to watch the spectacle and cheer on the children. Were they to join in the stoning we would not have a chance.

The children chant,

> *Yanqui run away or die today!*
> *Yanqui run away or die today!*
> *Yanqui run away or die today!*
> *Yanqui run away or die today!*

I now notice that they wear green T-shirts with a red eagle's head on them and something written in Spanish. The shirts remind me of the class T-shirts worn by students at the high school where I teach. Watching the children I recall the crazed children in Golding's *The Lord of the Flies* celebrating their victorious pig-hunting expedition, chanting *Kill the Beast! Cut his throat! Spill his blood.*

Continuing on as fast as Anne is able we finally leave our neighborhood, or what used to be our neighborhood, and continue to walk along a street separated from the houses on each side by two high cinderblock walls that are now covered with Graffiti. Nevertheless I appreciate the protection the creepily defaced walls provide. The street is thankfully vacant of pedestrians. Cars pass by occasionally, their passengers staring dully at us. We're relieved that we can stop and rest for a moment. We stand about exhausted feeling like survivors of a shark attack standing on the beach and looking at one another in a daze. But unlike the survivors of the shark attack we are still in the water like in the movie *Open Water* so it's impossible to relax. *Drive-by shooters* come to my mind but I say nothing. The wound on Anne's face has clotted but still oozes small drops of bright red blood. Her face looks as if she has been in a car accident and is heartbreaking to see. Though Kelly is holding herself together the expression on her face makes it clear that she is devastated by what has happened to her mother.

"Do you think you can continue on?" I ask Anne.

"I don't think I have any choice, do I, Jeffrey?" she replies stubbornly. "We're in the middle of a zero-sum game. If we stay here we'll definitely end up on the zero side of the equation."

"Then we better continue on," I say.

Ten minutes or so later we reach a busy intersection with a light. I'm thinking that perhaps we could get a ride with someone. So as we wait for the light to turn green, I go over to the first car also waiting for the light to change. I am thinking I'll offer to pay them for a ride but as I approach the car I see two brown faces staring back at me. As I walk by I look into the passenger window. The woman stares at me. I quickly hurry on to the car behind. But its driver is also Hispanic and gives me an angry look and waves me on. I try one more. Again a man and woman are sitting in the front seat. The man looks at me and smiles an Arsenio smile and gestures for me to get in. The woman wiggles her tongue at me and I step back in horror.

I imagine that somewhere in Mexico a corporation with a name like *Biovasion* is cloning tens of thousands of Arsenios and Imeldas. I back up against a chain-link fence surrounding a weed-infested lot with a dilapidated gas station on it. It's closed I assume because of leaky storage tanks that poison the soil below. The light has turned green and I look through the windows of the cars as they pass by. They're all Hispanic. *Where are my people?* For the first time I despair that we might not escape the Hispanic nightmare that had suddenly come upon us. I walk back to Anne and Kelly feeling very much like Willy Loman must have felt when he realized his American dream had become a personal nightmare from which he could not escape.

"What's wrong, Jeffrey?" Anne asks in a worried tone of voice. Recently she has been so angry with me, more than angry really. But she doesn't want me to fall apart. We're still a family.

"No luck. Come on, let's get going," I say to her, seeing in her eyes that she knows I'm keeping some bad news to myself.

The street we must cross is a wide avenue and before we are halfway the light turns yellow. We run for the median, fearing the worst if caught in the open. The traffic is heavy and swooshes by so we don't dare try to cross against the red light and risk ending up as roadkill. Besides we're too exhausted to attempt to sprint to the other side. Along the median is a fence and as we wait for the light to change I notice a jerrybuilt shrine made of candles, plastic flowers, pinwheels, deflated balloons lying limp on the asphalt, and photos attached to a big sheet of paper. Anymore these makeshift memorials seem to be everywhere. Apparently putting them anywhere a family member has been killed is a Hispanic tradition. In this case I assume a child was run over on the way to or from school.

Personally I hate the things. They give me the creeps. I mean that's what we have cemeteries for. But mostly I resent them because they have become so prolific in recent years that they are a constant reminder of how America has become a Hispanic nation. Given the daily drive-by shootings I imagine that the barrios must be littered with them. I wonder why the authorities allow them to exist but bureaucratic indifference doesn't surprise me. The light takes forever so I decide to take a closer look and as I approach the memorial I think I'll rip the thing from the fence and throw the objects into the street. I bend down to see the photos. What I see almost knocks me back into the street. The photos are of skulls and flowers and a crucifix with the skulls painted on it. Most shocking is that Anne, Kelly, and I are in the photos. In one Kelly wears a red dress decorated with grotesquely smiling skulls and from the sleeves extend two bony arms. Beneath the photos is written **Dia de los Muertos**. *FUCK! What is going on? How can this be?* I stand up and quickly return to Anne and Kelly.

"What is that?" Anne asks. "You look like you've seen a ghost."

"Nothing, nothing at all. The light's green. Let's go." We hurry across the street.

Once we are on the other side, Anne asks, "Jeffrey, where are the suitcases?"

"Don't you remember? We left them where you were hit by a rock. They don't matter anyway. They would only slow us down. Come on, baby." As I speak I feel terrified that Anne might be losing it.

"That's right. I remember now, Jeffrey. I'm sorry. I'm just tired."

"You're doing great, baby. Come on." For the first time since our nightmare began she looks at me tenderly. If she is still angry about what I allowed to happen to Kelly she isn't showing it. She also knows I love Kelly no less than she and that I'll be haunted for the rest of my life for my failure to be the father I should have been, to be there when my child most needed me. And now it seems our little family is struggling to survive.

We continue on our way. The sun is directly overhead and beating down mercilessly. I keep expecting to see a police car or an ambulance, but no luck. Though it is clear that Anne has been injured, no one stops, and considering the situation perhaps that's for the best. It seems we are on our own and I'm beginning to despair. *Are we completely surrounded by hostile aliens?* I recall the *Resident Evil* video game in which Leon the young American special agent is sent to rescue the president's daughter who has been kidnapped and carried off to a zombie-infested country. Our situation is different. It's our homes and communities, not us, that have been kidnapped.

I chuckle grimly to myself thinking that were we relatives of President Bush there would be helicopters and an elite force of black-clad commandos arriving to rescue us. But we're just ordinary citizens, not members of that wealthy, politically powerful inner circle. And I am no well-armed superhero like Leon. Our only hope is to find somewhere other Americans like ourselves. I have to keep believing for Anne and Kelly's sake that we will.

About an hour later we arrive at what was once a 7-Eleven mini-mart and hurry in to get out of the sun and to get something to eat and drink. Inside though we discover it isn't a 7-Eleven at all but a Mexican store, a bodega. Most of the merchandise is Mexican and the labels and signs are in Spanish. It's less hot inside but still warm and muggy. No air conditioning. I buy bottles of water, a package of cookies, a box of bandages, antiseptic cream, and a small package of tissues from the heavy-set, stolid Mexican woman who conducts the transaction in silence. A Hispanic man in his late twenties or early thirties who was stocking shelves when we entered watches us the entire time we're in the store. Neither he nor the woman shows any interest in Anne's condition but simply watches us as if we might steal something if given the chance. I'm thinking that perhaps we do look pretty desperate.

After getting what we need we quickly leave the store though we dread having to face the heat. Outside I lead Anne to a lamppost at the corner of the small parking lot and have her sit on the concrete base. Kelly stands between the sun and her mother in order to keep Anne's face in the shade. I open the package of tissues, soak a few in water, and gently wipe the blood from her face.

"It's pretty bad, huh Dad?"

"It looks worse than it really is," I say, not wanting to alarm her.

The rock had opened a jagged-edged cut below Anne's right eye. The wound is caked with dried blood. *Thank God* it hadn't hit her eye or temple which would have either blinded her in one eye or killed her. I clean her face and the wound the best I can. I don't want to disturb it too much and cause it to bleed again. I apply some of the antiseptic cream and put on a bandage.

During the process Anne watches me affectionately, occasionally glancing up at Kelly and giving her a reassuring smile.

"Here, drink some water," I say handing the bottle to her. I then give Kelly a bottle of water and pass out some of the cookies. I open the remaining bottle and take a couple of swallows. While eating one of the cookies I study the sign in front of the store. The former ELE**7**VEN has been whitewashed and replaced with a red, crudely painted CIN**5**CO. I turn to Kelly who is taking a long drink from her bottle.

"Kelly, look at the sign, the 7-eleven has been replaced by 5-*cinco*. I believe 7-eleven means *open from 7 a.m. to 11 p.m.* But 5 to 5 doesn't make any sense, does it? What do you think?"

"It probably means *Cinco de Mayo*, the fifth of May," she says matter-of-factly.

"God, I bet you're right." *Are all the 7-Elevens in the country now Cinco-de-Mayos? What a distressing thought!*

"But you should see this, Dad," Kelly calls over from where she's looking at the side of the store. I walk over to see and find written on the side of the wall:

Salsa Zone: Gringos keep out!

"That's swell, huh, Dad?"

"Yeah, really swell," I say glumly.

I walk back to Anne and ask her how she's doing. "I'm all right," she says, but I can see that she really isn't all right. I put my hand on her shoulder but say nothing. What can I say? *I blew it.*

"Well guys, should we rest a few minutes longer before going on?" I ask.

"No way, Dad. I want to keep going until we reach someplace with people like us."

"She's right, Jeffrey."

"Okay, let's continue then."

As we continue on I think about Kelly's translation of 5-*cinco* and ask her about the shirts worn by the children who threw rocks at us.

"Kelly, those kids. Did you see what was written on their T-shirts?"

"You mean *HECHO EN MEXICO*?"

"Yeah, that's it. What does that mean?"

"Made in Mexico."

"Weird," I say. "Most likely they were or at least they were conceived in Mexico," I say to lighten the mood a little.

"You're very clever, pops," she says with a grin.

"Not as clever as you, darlin'," I tell her, thinking it was really true. In her own way Kelly is a hell of a lot wiser than I am.

After that we continue on pretty much in silence trying to conserve our remaining energy. My legs feel like rubber. I'm thoroughly exhausted and I know why. That fucking Imelda. A combination of Circe and Delilah she had sapped all my strength. She defeated me.

As we continue our journey I begin to feel uncertain of its destination. *What if America no longer exists?* What if it has become an **Ahmarika** or **Azterica** or **Amexica**? What if we have become like those characters in horror movies like *Dawn of the Dead* or *Resident Evil: Apocalypse*, whose familiar and comfortable worlds become overnight threatening alien environments. *I must stop thinking this shit and try to be positive. Damn it! I've got to think of Anne and Kelly.*

Out of the blue I hear myself saying in a bullish tone of voice, "Not much farther guys. A mile or so and we'll reach the freeway. I'm sure we'll find some Americans in the area, maybe even meet up with some who are in the same situation we're in." I look at Anne and Kelly. Though each makes an effort to show some optimism what comes through most is their wretchedness. I turn away so they don't see my own discouragement.

During this leg of the journey the walking becomes easier as we descend downhill toward the freeway. I just let gravity pull me forward. Midway down the hill the street curves so that we can see the freeway and bay in the distance.

"There's the freeway, Dad!" Kelly says excitedly.

"That's right, baby," I reply, but my heart sinks hearing her desperate enthusiasm. Besides I'm not at all sure that getting to the freeway will help us.

At the bottom of the hill we stop completely exhausted. Kelly sits down on the sidewalk while Anne paces nervously back and forth. There used to be a liquor store on the corner but it too had become a bodega. On the side of the wall is written in giant graffiti:

Haz patria, mata un gringo!

We look at one another without saying anything.

"Kelly," I finally ask, "what does that say?"

She looks at me with a frightened expression, her eyes opened wide. At first she doesn't seem to want to tell me. Then she says, "I think it says *Be patriotic, kill a gringo.*" She turns to her mother. That's how children figure out how bad a situation is. They look to their parents. Anne responds with a sad smile and says, "It's just to scare us, honey. That's all. They won't..." Anne doesn't complete her sentence. She was about to say *They won't hurt us*. But she can't say that to Kelly. How can she?

Turning to me, Kelly asks, "Dad, is that right? It's just to scare us?"

I walk over to her and put my arm around her and say, "Your mother is right, baby. The sign just means that we are not welcome. It's like the graffiti gangs use to tell members of other gangs to stay out of their neighborhood. That's all."

"But gangs do kill."

"That's true but only if you ignore their graffiti and we're not. We're leaving. They can see that. Besides, remember when we used to drive to New Mexico to see your uncle and grandmother. Each time we entered a small town a sign would say *Welcome to Kingman* or *Welcome to Gallup*, and when we left the town a sign would say *Leaving Kingman* or *Leaving Gallup*. That's what this sign means, that we are leaving and are now out of harm's way. So, you don't have to worry anymore. Okay?"

"Okay, Dad." I look closely at her to see if my words have reassured her. She smiles a little. Yes, it's better. A father's words are like magic. *Or was her smile to reassure me?*

Having no idea of what the reception will be I go into the store to buy three more bottles of water. Kelly and Anne prefer to stay out in the heat. A middle-aged man and a woman stand behind the counter. They look like man and wife. And as I expected they are both Hispanic. I get the water and walk toward the counter. We are strangers to one another. I realize then that we will always be strangers to one another. We will always watch each other suspiciously, just as the slaves and their masters had, just as the Indians and the white man had, and now our turn has come to be a minority living in an alien culture that we will never trust.

I recall the scene where the creature in Mary Shelley's *Frankenstein* says to Victor Frankenstein, *"You are my creator but I am your master."* Americans had once been masters and now they are being vanquished, becoming refugees in their own country. Were this couple black Americans I would go to them as fellow Americans and ask for their help. They would understand even better than white Americans what it means to be strangers in their own land. I would feel a bond with them. I would feel at home with them but they too seem to be no more.

I pay at the counter and ask for some change so that I can use the pay phone outside.

"It don't work," says the man, who places on the counter a dollar bill, two dimes, and a few pennies.

"Can you give me change for the dollar so I can at least try?" I ask.

"We cannot spare the change," he says indignantly.

"May I use your phone?" I say, mostly just to annoy him and to hear his response.

"It's against policy, Señor."

I hate that word *Señor*. I hate all Spanish words. They have become like the drops of poison the Renaissance Italians, who were apparently master poisoners, would place in the ear of their sleeping victims. I turn and walk away but stop at the door and look back at my two antagonists. "Where are you from?" I ask.

"Mexico, Señor. We are *mejicanos,"* he says with a broad smile, his wife nodding in agreement.

Finally, I can't contain myself and blurt out, "Why are you here in my country?"

"Because we love America, gringo," says the woman, the man nodding in agreement, but no longer smiling.

I let out a huff of resentment and walk outside and give Anne and Kelly each a bottle of water. As I look into their faces I realize that were I alone none of this would matter. Maybe I would have killed the two people in the store and then walk to the train tracks and step in front of the train. Suicide would be easy. What is unbearable is to think that Anne and Kelly depend upon a piece of shit like me and all the other pieces of white shit that have failed them. They will go anywhere I take them without question, even Anne who must think at times that what I'm doing makes little sense.

I have always thought of women as the wiser sex of our species but in desperate times, usually resulting from the foolish, greedy, or vicious behavior of men, they trustingly surrender themselves to an irrational faith in the goodness and wisdom of men. No God could have allowed women to be part of such a cruel tragedy. Even Imelda is more victim than victimizer.

"We're almost there, guys. Let's go," I tell the girls in a faux cheerful tone, thinking to myself, *Where? Where is there? Where in the fuck am I taking them?"*

We continue on. We hurry across a street that runs parallel to the freeway and make our way up and over the railroad tracks. For a moment I consider the possibility of hopping a train but then realize that if we caught a train going south we would be heading toward the Mexican border and if we caught one going north we would be heading toward Los Angeles. No, the train is out, too dangerous and futile.

On the other side of the tracks we enter a narrow thickly wooded strip of land that parallels the freeway for about a quarter of a mile. It's about a hundred yards wide and consists mostly of eucalyptus trees. It's cool in the shade of the trees and I feel it would be nice to rest here an hour or so, but we are on our own and I want to find a place to stay before nightfall. Nevertheless we take our time passing through the trees.

"Jeffrey!" Anne whispers.

"What is it?" I respond. Anne nods toward a man and a woman. I had not noticed them in the shadows. Both are shabbily dressed and very rough looking. The man wears a San Diego Padres baseball cap. Apparently they are homeless.

"Hello, partner." The man says to me.

"Hi," I respond cautiously.

"Could you spare some change? We haven't eaten in a while. Don't worry, we don't intend you any harm."

"Sure, I think I have a little money I can give you." I take out a five-dollar bill and give it to the man. "I wish I could give you more."

"I understand, though five dollars more would be most helpful. Anymore, panhandling isn't easy. The new people don't give a damn about us and the streets are dangerous."

I only have a dollar bill, a ten, and two twenties. So I give him the ten but am reluctant to ask for the five back.

"Thank you. Here, take your five. Ten dollars is all we need. It ain't for food. We'll buy whiskey and share with a few of our friends.

"How do you eat then?" I ask.

"Garbage mostly. We do our shopping at night in the dumpsters and trash cans," he says in a wry, humorless tone of voice.

"You say there are others?'

"Oh yeah." Then he nods toward the length of the wood. "Do you see?"

I look carefully among the shadows and begin to see people sitting on the ground or standing by the trees. Silently they stare at us.

I turn to the man and say, "I don't have much money."

"Don't worry, mister. We appreciate your kindness. They won't bother you. They know your situation. Most have gone through the same thing."

"I don't understand. What do mean by *our situation*?"

"You're fleeing, right?"

"Yes, but how did you know that?"

"Look at your poor missus. All bloodied. You were attacked weren't you?"

"Yes."

"Rock-throwers would be my guess. Kids."

"How do you know that?"

"Because you're here. Had they been older, they would have used bats and pipes and you wouldn't be here now. We see people like you each day. Some stop here to rest and tend to their wounds. Some stay among us but not many because there's only so much garbage available in the area. Some continue on to the river and go east. Those too old to go on or too seriously wounded stay. Many die. I don't know what happens to others. None have ever returned for those left behind. Some cross to the other side of the freeway like you're going to try to do, right?"

"We're not sure."

"Well if you do, be careful. We've seen a number of refugees hit by cars. The drivers don't seem to care and they never stop. You're just game to many of them."

"Refugees? What do you mean by that?"

"You're fleeing, looking for refuge, aren't you? Looking for safety among your own people, right?"

"Yes... I suppose we are. Do you know what is happening? I still don't understand."

"You cannot stay in your home because strangers have moved in. Isn't that right?"

"Yes."

"And you cannot stay in you neighborhood because there are strangers there also. Very unfriendly strangers. Right?"

"Yes, that's right."

"That's the story we get from the people who have been coming here recently. They are not like the homeless who were here before, people who drank too much or got into drugs or just fell on hard times and couldn't cope any longer. The new people are just ordinary folks like you. That's all we know. Like I said, the others never returned so I don't know if they found what they were looking for. It's why we hide here during the day and go out only at night, though it is also dangerous at night. Lots of drive-by shootings at night. I'd say you people have been pretty lucky so far. And none of us knows how long we'll be able to stay here."

"You said that some people die?"

"Sure, lots do."

"What do you do with them, their bodies?"

"At night we take the bodies to the dumpsters."

"God that's awful." Anne and Kelly had walked to the edge of the trees near the freeway, apparently afraid of the strange people dwelling among the shadows of the trees. I'm glad they couldn't hear what the man is telling me. I wish he hadn't told me but think it's better to know what we are up against.

"We don't have any choice. Otherwise this place would become a graveyard. Plus the dogs would get into them. You're right. It is awful. Everything is awful."

"And what are you going to do?"

"Exist. That's all we do, just exist. When one of us gets killed *out there* the authorities come and take the body away as if it were the body of a dog or cat or a possum or skunk run over by a car. They don't come here though. We are anonymous. We exist but we don't exist. Barbara and me, she's my companion, we manage. By the way my name is John," he says holding out his hand.

"Jeffrey, I'm Jeffrey. Glad to meet you, John," I say, amazed at what I'm hearing and witnessing.

"We feel sorry for people like you who have children to care for. That burden must be unbearable."

His companion approaches and stands by his side. Like his, her brown, weatherworn face suggests years of homelessness. Her gaunt features and desperate look remind me of the women in the photographs of the Great

Depression taken by Dorothea Lange and Walker Evans. Only her eyes seem undiminished by the elements but even they express hardship and fear.

"I guess I ought to be going."

"Good luck, Jeffrey, and look after the missus and young'un."

"Thanks," I say and walk to where Anne and Kelly are waiting for me. They watch me as I approach. Pondering what John has just told me I feel totally depressed.

When I join them Anne says, "What are we going to do now, Jeffrey? This looks pretty crazy to me." The usual critical tone of voice is absent. She's frightened.

"I'm going to try to hitch a ride. Wait here."

Reaching the freeway's edge I realize I underestimated the speed of the cars. *How could anyone stop for a hitchhiker?* Then I think, *Of course the emergency phones!* I go back and tell Anne and Kelly of my idea. We only need to walk along the freeway until we reach the phone, or if we are lucky, until the Highway Patrol sees us and stops.

So we begin walking in single file. I lead the way with Kelly and then Anne following. The whooshing of the cars is nerve-rackingly loud. Then a car gives a long loud honk as it passes scaring us half to death. The car sounds as if it is coming right at us. And then another car honks and another and another—each time startling us, the sound trailing off in the distance. It is as if we are being shot at and I worry that being shot at is a possibility since freeway shootings had been increasing even before our neighborhood was invaded. But I'm thinking the honkers are hardly better than the shooters. They're both cruel motherfuckers. I wonder whether their behavior is connected to everything else that has occurred. Had things been going wrong for a long time and Americans just didn't want to see it, preferring to sit in a darkened room before the glow of the television, eating their pizza and swilling their beer, pretending that the pounding at the door was just the wind?

I look back at Kelly and Anne. Anne is weeping holding her hand over her mouth so that Kelly won't hear though the traffic noise would have prevented that. Kelly looks frightened and exhausted. *She won't last much longer.* She's keeping it all inside but it's clear that she's at the breaking point. *I must hold myself together!*

Twenty minutes later we come to an emergency phone. The box is scribbled with graffiti apparently with a black felt pen. I open the door of the box—the phone is missing. Someone had cut the wire and taken the phone. Desperation sweeps over me and fearing the look on their faces I hesitate to look back at Anne and Kelly.

What in the fuck am I doing? I've brought my wife and daughter to the edge of a freeway. What did I expect we could do here? For just one second I consider running out into the river of honking cars. *No!* I will not commit suicide. I will kill first, kill in order to save my girls.

We'll go back to the street we crossed earlier and I will use the knife that I still have with me to car-jack someone. We have just suffered a house-jacking and I would feel no remorse taking someone's car especially not from *one of them*. For Anne and Kelly I would even kill one of *them* if he or she tried to stop me. That is just the way it is now. *Welcome to Baghdad, America.* As Arsenio has just proven to me, it's a Darwinian world no different in America than in Iraq, Afghanistan, Darfur, Somalia or any of those other places where tribes and clans attack and kill one another.

But then I think of Anne and Kelly seeing me kill someone and stealing his or her car, becoming a murderer, a thief, an outlaw. They couldn't accept that even if it meant that their lives would be saved. They may live in a Darwinian world but they are not part of it. It is a world in which they are truly the aliens. I decide that we should go back to the place among the trees where John and Barbara are and rest there for a while but that option also seems frightening. I then recall the story about Odysseus' crew in the land of the lotus-eaters that Arsenio told his nightmarish son Lope about. There we would not escape the hellish world that has suddenly enveloped us. To the contrary we would remain its prisoners.

"Daddy, Daddy, a hot air balloon!" Kelly yells, snapping me out of my own lotus-like stupor. I turn to her to find her blue eyes shining with joy. *My heart breaks. What have I done?* I haven't seen her like this since she was a little girl, her face filled with joy as we approached the entrance of the Del Mar Fair or Disneyland. That seems so long ago.

"You're not looking, Daddy."

I turn to where she is pointing. "Yes, I am, darling, yes I am."

On the other side of the freeway is a beautiful gay-looking rainbow colored hot-air balloon tethered in a dirt field about the size of a baseball diamond.

"It's *very* beautiful, huh Daddy?"

"Yes, baby, it's very beautiful." I look to Anne. She wears a sad smile. She was always the practical one and I can see that she thinks we are wasting precious time. The sun is descending toward the horizon and it will be dark soon. I smile and feel a jolt of despair course through my body. I look back to the balloon.

"Can we go in it, Daddy? *Please.*"

Years ago while visiting my mother and brother in Albuquerque we rode in a hot-air balloon during the hot-air balloon festival. The balloon was attached to a long rope so that we went only a couple of hundred feet into the air. Anne and Kelly enjoyed the ride but I felt claustrophobic and talked with the operator to keep my mind off being in the small basket-like gondola so high above the ground. The operator was pleased by my interest in the contraption and explained at great length how it worked.

Suddenly I think *I can fly that balloon! If it were a jet plane there would be no chance, but I can fly that balloon.* It's a crazy idea but being reasonable doesn't seem to be an option any longer. It just may be an escape from all this madness.

"Hey guys, I have an idea," I yell, because of the noise coming from the freeway, "but I will tell you what it is once we're on the other side of the freeway. So let's go back to the street we came from and cross over to the other side."

Kelly walks over and puts her arms around me and looking up says, "Daddy, I don't want to go back."

"Why, baby? We're going to get out of this mess very soon."

"I know, Daddy, but I don't think I can go much farther. My stomach hurts bad."

"Okay, baby. Let me think." I stand for a moment looking at the nightmarish freeway and then toward the wood that we just came from which now appears minuscule in the distance. I notice a warning sign with a father, mother, and child running across the freeway. Is that possible or would one or all of us be killed trying to dash across? The freeway seems inhuman, a great concrete, asphalt serpent that slithers across the landscape. Its blood cells are made of metal, rubber, plastic, and human flesh. It is indifferent to all forms of life except itself, which is an alien form of life. With the same indifference it kills a dog or cat, a possum or skunk, a coyote or fox, or a father, mother, or child, and it does so each day by the thousands across the nation. John had just said that people trying to cross the freeway were treated no better than rabbit or dog trying to cross. As I contemplate my own family's crossing, my blood turns to ice water. If Anne or Kelly are injured or killed, then I will have failed. And if I am killed the outcome might be the same if my death caused Anne and Kelly to lose hope and give up. Alone in a cruel world they would soon become its victims.

Kelly is still standing by my side, still believing dads can do anything. Anne waits somberly for my decision. A horn sounds and then another. *The beast is taunting us.* I speak to Kelly.

"Honey, I am going to tell you my idea. I want to go up in that balloon. Would you like that?"

"Oh yes, Daddy, I would."

"But the shortest way to it is across the freeway." I look to Anne. She is shaking her head as if to say, *No, Jeffrey,* but she says nothing. She knows we are desperate and that Kelly is very close to the breaking point. Kelly looks happy but I'm certain that inside she's as fragile as a snowflake. And Anne doesn't want to cut the thread of happiness that has enabled Kelly to smile because I believe Anne thought she'd never again see Kelly happy.

"It will be very dangerous," I say to Kelly, "and you will have to run very fast. What do you think?" She listens to me and then looks at the big, rainbow-colored balloon standing in the distance like a giant exotic flower. Her eyes are wide open as if she were seeing a vision of the Virgin.

"Yes, Daddy. Let's go across the freeway."

I turn to Anne who has joined us creating a huddle of three. "What do you think?"

"I dare not say what I think. I will do whatever you two decide."

"Okay, we'll sprint together to the center divider. We'll hold hands to stay together."

"I don't think we should," says Kelly. "I can run faster with my arms free."

"Okay, maybe you're right." Kelly's young and athletic, and I'm sure she's capable of outrunning me and Anne.

"Anne," I say, "I don't think you should try it in those pumps. Take them off and run barefoot. I'll put your shoes in my shirt." The image of Anne tripping and falling flashes through my mind. *God!* I can't make the idea go away so I relegate it to my mental penalty box where it and all the other fears must wait their turn to torment me. I take Anne's shoes and stuff them into my shirt. As I do I look at the bandaged face that I love so much. Anne's hair is matted from hours of perspiring and her eyes are red and swollen from crying silently. *We must do this!* flashes through my mind like lightning.

"We can do this, honey," I say gently, wanting to say more, but feeling I have cheapened my words by failing to protect my family.

"I hope so," she responds, each word filled with uncertainty. *Oh, Anne! What have I done?* Then I answer the question: *I have allowed harm that cannot be undone—ever.*

We line up along the freeway like the sprinters in the Olympics. We don't have to run far, but we are running for our lives. Watching the traffic I consider slowing it down or even stopping some of it by throwing rocks at the cars and causing an accident but then realize that such an idea only shows how far my mental state has deteriorated.

"Okay, guys," I say, "run when I say *go*. Keep your eyes on the traffic. If you must stop... never mind." I wait. I'm hoping that the traffic will come in waves but it doesn't. It's just heavy enough to make getting across all four lanes seem impossible and light enough for the cars to travel at full speed. If we try to sprint across all four lanes, one or all of us will be killed.

"I tell you what, we're going to run across the first two lanes and stop on the second line and wait for a chance to cross the other two lanes. That way we'll only have to worry about two lanes at a time."

"That sounds pretty crazy, Jeffrey. What if someone changes lanes?"

I hadn't thought of that but say only, "Let's hope that doesn't happen. These people don't want to run us over. They will try to avoid us if they can" though I no longer really believe that. Now I believe some would enjoy turning us into roadkill and if they did swerve to avoid us it would be to protect their cars not us. Anne echoes my thought.

"A few days ago I would have agreed with you, Jeffrey."

"Daddy, let's just go. All this talking is making me nervous."

"Okay, baby, okay. Two lanes first, then stop on the line unless I say go." I wait until I can see an opening approach in the first two lanes. Kelly decides to hold my hand rather than go it alone. As she does I recall what I used to say to her at an intersection during our walks when she was a little girl. *Stop, look, and listen. Stop, look, and listen.* That seems so long ago. And now I know what I then only vaguely understood, that Kelly's childhood was a magical time. It still is.

"*GO!*" I feel my hand jerk Kelly as I dart forward. I can see three or four cars only seconds away. "*STOP!*" I yell, but they didn't need to be told. We stand on the middle line, the traffic behind and in front of us whooshing by, horns blaring unbearably. They're not warning us, but venting their anger. *Assholes!* Then I think *what a stupid idea this is.* But now there is no going back. I see an opening appear up ahead, watch it quickly approach, then yell, *"GO!"*

"We made it, Daddy," Kelly says excitedly, still tightly holding my hand. "We're getting pretty good at this." I look down into her face and smile. I don't know what to think, except that *my daughter's a miracle.*

"Yeah we did. Let's get over this divider." All three of us climb over the divider which is, thank God, just a concrete barrier a few feet high. While I catch my breath, I look at the faces as they whizz by. *I hate them all. They're all adversaries.* In the southbound lanes the cars are fewer and strung out over a longer distances.

"The traffic isn't as bad on this side," I yell, "but keep your eyes on the cars in case one changes lanes. And if I say stop, stop." We wait. My heart is still beating fast. I realize it's not because I'm out of breath but because of the terror I feel standing in the middle of the freeway with my wife and daughter, fearing that my little family might be destroyed. This time I decide to wait however long it takes for a big break in the traffic. *Where are the cops when you need them?* Finally the traffic thins enough for us to give it a try.

"Get ready! Hold hands! But be ready to stop! *GO!*" We run across the nearest three lanes, and I yell *STOP!* to let two cars pass. A couple of horns blare, but we're not trapped in traffic as before. *"GO!"* We dart across the final lane and keep on running until we reach a seven-foot chain-link fence and stop. I look in both directions for an opening. None. *Fuck!* Then Kelly says, "I'll go first," and climbs over the fence like a monkey. Impressed by what we have just witnessed, Anne and I look at each other and smile.

"Come-on, guys! It's not that hard."

"Maybe not for you but we're coming," I say.

While Anne holds to the fence I put on her shoes. As I do, I see small lacerations on the bottoms of her feet. I then help her up the fence the best I can. As she begins to climb down the other side, her skirt gets hung up on the top of the fence.

"Hold on, Anne! Your dress is caught," I say and reach up to unhook it. Kelly reaches up to help support her mother while I free the dress from the fence.

"Hold on, Mom," Kelly says to her. "You don't what to lose your dress. That would really be embarrassing." Anne looks down at Kelly and smiles. I hate what Anne is being put through and say nothing.

Once Anne is on the other side I take out the knife I still have with me, stick it through the fence, and climb upward. I feel decrepit as I struggle to pull my body to the top of the wavering fence. *You fucking piece of shit!* I think. At the top of the fence I see the colorful balloon. I can't imagine a more cheerful expression of hope. *Keep your focus on the balloon and your family, stupid. Yes, that's what I must do.* On the other side I hesitate to pick up the knife. I hate the damn thing. But then I think, *You silly ass! Don't you understand the world has changed?* So I pick it up and stick it between my belt and pants.

The two girls look at me, waiting. "Well," I say, "let's take a look at that balloon," and we start walking toward it like awed tourists approaching an Egyptian sphinx. I look about to see if someone is guarding it. If there is, what will I do? Will I use the knife? I see no one. *Weird.* I have the crazy idea that that the balloon has been waiting just for us. Kelly glances up at me. She's exhausted but smiling and excited. *There's nothing in the world better,* I think to myself, *than seeing your child happy.* Yet it seems I had forgotten that until I saw her very unhappy.

I never fully appreciated how much Anne's and Kelly's happiness meant to me. They are my *raison d'être* as the French say, my reason for being. I never fully realized how important they were until I saw them suffering and afraid. I understand now what life is really all about—the ones you love. I recall a French movie showing how emperor penguin couples suffer all sorts of Antarctic hazards in order to give birth to their only child. For two months the male stands in the darkness of winter without eating, the egg containing his child balanced on his webbed feet, tucked beneath a warm blanket of his skin, and the couple deeply loving one another during the time allotted to them. Our world has become like that of the penguins, cold and filled with predators, and like the penguins we seek safety among our own kind. But unlike the penguin fathers I failed my responsibility to my child. Now I can only hope that soon we shall be encircled by our own people for they are the only ones to whom we can turn.

We cross a street and continue toward the balloon. To the north the bay comes into view. The sun is the color of red coral and has swollen to a large disk a few inches above the horizon. As we near the balloon I expect to see somebody but no one is about. Once we reach the basket-like gondola of the balloon Anne gives me an incredulous look.

"What are you thinking?" I ask.

"At this point," she says, "it's probably better not to think too much." I have to agree. The gondola of the balloon is as small as I remember and the balloon itself hangs above us like a giant mythical creature, beautiful but scary. Right away Kelly clambers in.

"Let's go, you guys," she says in a buoyant tone of voice that I would have thought impossible for anyone who's gone through what we have gone through the past few days, especially Kelly, who suffered so much. That thought and the accompanying guilt make it impossible for me to share her happiness. However I'm grateful to see a smile on her face. I help Anne into the gondola, and then untie the ropes and climb in. I pull the handle on the torch which releases a roaring tongue of yellow flame causing the balloon to give an upward tug to the gondola.

"Daddy, Daddy. Look!" Kelly screams. I look about, frightened that someone is coming. "What is it? I don't see anyone."

"A dog!" I look to where Kelly is pointing and before I can stop her she climbs out of the gondola and runs toward a small dog that seems to have appeared from nowhere. The balloon continues to creep upward and I am afraid that Anne and I will have to jump out because I haven't yet figured out how to make the balloon descend. The thought of our not escaping is unbearable.

For the moment all Anne and I do is watch and yell to Kelly to hurry. When she reaches the dog she falls to her knees and the dog immediately jumps into her lap as if she were its owner.

Behind me I hear Anne's moaning, "Oh God, oh God. Jeffrey we need to get out."

"It's okay, it's okay. We still have some time," I say, not feeling so sure. The balloon is a couple of feet off the ground and is moving away from Kelly. I yell to Kelly to hurry, while Anne screams out her name. *Goddamn dog!*

Kelly doesn't pay us any attention and now Anne is insisting that she's getting out. I tell her that we're not going to leave Kelly behind and that we'll both get out when I say so. I fear though Anne's going to ignore me and suddenly climb out just as Kelly did. I understand now that the relationship between a mother and her child is a paradox. One would expect it to be similar to that existing between a smaller child-like satellite revolving around the larger parent body. But that expectation comes from viewing the relationship from the outside, the child *appearing* to be less significant than her adult mother, but that's not at all the way a mother experiences the relationship. The force that draws her to her child is like the force that holds the moon about the earth, the earth about the sun. That's just the way it is. And I know that at some critical point nothing could stop Anne from jumping out of the gondola.

After what seems an eternity Kelly stands up and begins to run toward the balloon, which is now a few feet off the ground. Anne begins yelling, begging Kelly to run faster, and as I watch I'm very much impressed by how fast my girl can run. In a moment she's below us walking quickly to stay up with the gondola, the bottom of which reaches just above her shoulders. I yell to Anne to hold my legs and then bend as far as I can over the side of the gondola. I yell at Kelly to let go of the dog and grab my hand, not even sure that I'm capable of pulling her up. Again I yell for Anne to hold on to me mostly to keep her from jumping out of the gondola and breaking a leg. What I feel inside is a combination of panic and despair. It seems all the fears have been released from the penalty box in my mind.

But Kelly doesn't grab for my hand, and I conclude that Anne and I need to get out of the gondola. *I've lost control of the situation!* Then Kelly does the most unexpected thing.

"Daddy! Catch the dog," she yells, now running to stay up with the balloon. I see that Kelly won't leave the dog behind. *Oh God!* I hear Anne say in a loud pleading voice, "Jeffrey, do something. Please. I'll forgive you everything if you get Kelly into the basket." *Oh God!*

Then it happens in the blink of an eye. Using all her strength and letting out a big grunt Kelly tosses the dog upward to me from between her legs as if she were shooting a free throw. At that moment my heart sinks. There won't be a second chance.

She *must* have used all her strength because the dog hits me in the face rather than in my arms and for a moment I juggle to get hold of the animal but finally I do and I put it on the floor of the gondola. *Jesus, I'm a nervous wreck.* By now the gondola is seven or eight feet above the ground and continuing to rise and pick up speed. There is no way that Kelly can reach it or me. I hear Anne, who is standing beside me, saying, "Oh no, oh no, oh God, no." I look briefly at her and see that she's going into shock. I look down at Kelly. I'm thinking we should jump out because in a few seconds it will be too late but Kelly hasn't panicked. She seems to know exactly what she's doing and I feel I can't do anything until she gives me some indication that I must. I'm waiting for her. Right now she's in control.

And it appears that she has had a plan all along because she grabs one of the dangling ropes. I'm now grateful I had not followed my first impulse which was to cut the ropes from the gondola. Kelly climbs upward, the rope swinging to and fro as she does. Once she's close enough, I grab her wrists and strain to pull her into the gondola. I'm impressed at how feeble I have become in middle age.

"Oh, thank God you're here, baby," Anne says, her eyes full of tears. She glances at me and I can see that for now I've been forgiven even though Kelly deserves all the credit and we are still stuck in a balloon that I know almost nothing about operating. I am only grateful to have my two girls back.

Kelly picks up the dog and gives it a big hung. It's strange how dogs can give kids something that no one else can. I think she feels better because she was able to focus on saving a little lost creature, allowing her to forget for a while all that has happened to her. At this moment she is not a victim but a hero.

"Can he come with us, Daddy?" she yells with delight.

"Oh, I think so after that dramatic rescue. And he can't weigh very much." I pull the handle to get the balloon moving upward. We ascend until we can see the horizon where the ocean and the sky meet. The carnelian sun is sinking into the horizon like a disappearing eye, one blind to the affairs of humanity. The San Diego River is mostly dry but on I-5 and I-8 the cars flow abundantly, streams of white and red lights. The lights of the houses of the neighborhoods that once had been so familiar to us flicker orange and yellow in the light of the setting sun. In the distance the buildings of downtown glimmer reddish orange. It all seems so familiar and beautiful yet now frighteningly strange.

I direct the balloon eastward.

"Where are we going, Daddy?"

"I'm not sure, Honey, but away from all this."

"Let's go to Kansas."

"Why there?" I ask.

"That's the home of Dorothy in *The Wizard of Oz*. The people seem awfully nice there and I think Toto and me would be happy there."

"Toto?"

"Yes," she says nodding to the little dog she holds in her arms.

"Well, then maybe that's where we should go, my beauty." *My little girl*, I thought. What has happened to my little girl? I can feel the tears wanting to come into my eyes but I won't let them. In her own way she is happy and I don't want to spoil it even though I'm thinking that the Kansas of *The Wizard of Oz* is not the Kansas of today, the Kansas of *In Cold Blood*, of a born-again Grand Inquisitor District Attorney pursuing abortionists and their desperate clientele, of meth labs, of Darwin haters, and of serial killers. I think a much happier place for Kelly would be Québec, Canada.

"Jeffrey, there is a lot of desert between us and anywhere. What if we get stuck in it?" I give Anne one of those *Not now!* looks she so often has given me. She understands immediately.

"If we land in the desert," I say, "the Minutemen will rescue us."

"Who are they, Daddy?"

"They are Americans looking out for Americans like us."

"Are you sure they will be there?"

"Yeah, baby, they'll be there if we need them."

"That's good," she says, now holding her mother tight with one arm and her dog with the other.

The sun has disappeared into the sea slowly taking with it the last illumination along the western horizon. Gradually we leave behind the twinkling plain of houses that extends inward from the shore, into foothills, finally dispersing into desert and the bluish black darkness. All is quiet except for the occasional roar of the torch that casts a brief yellowish orange glow upon the four travelers, the three humans looking downward at the receding congregations of homes and sparse automobiles traveling in the distance. Then we come upon something quite remarkable and most terrifying.

"What are those lights, Daddy?" Kelly asks, pointing to the south. I look and what I see are a dozen long dimly flickering columns. At first I'm puzzled then realize that they're columns of people, thousands of people carrying lights of all kinds, flashlights, lanterns, torches, slowly moving north and northeast in the pattern of an open fan. Farther off, the flickering lines look like slowly moving narrow streams of molten lava. Closer to us can be seen campfires scattered on either side the columns, apparently where some of the travelers are resting a while before continuing on.

"I'm not sure, Honey," I say, though I'm certain of what I am witnessing.

"We're going lower, Jeffrey," says Anne nervously so I pull the handle of the torch and as I do her face is illuminated. She has the look of a frightened animal.

"The lines are people walking, Dad."

"You're right, Honey. That's what they are."

"Are those the Minutemen?"

"Yes, honey, I believe so." I pull the handle again and again until we can see only filaments of light approaching all along the southwest. Suddenly the night grows cold and unfriendly and I feel terrified and depressed.

CPSIA information can be obtained at www.ICGtesting.com
Printed in the USA
BVOW09s1221030216

435313BV00005B/36/P